FAMILY

An Ursula Nordstrom Book

Also by John Donovan

FAMILY

a novel by

JOHN DONOVAN

HARPER & ROW, PUBLISHERS
New York, Hagerstown, San Francisco, London

Library of Congress Catalog Card Number: 75-37409

Trade ISBN 0-06-021721-9

Harpercrest ISBN 0-06-021722-7

FIRST EDITION

FAMILY

1
THE EXPERIMENT

TIME is not supposed to matter to me. It's important to humans because they place things in time: it happened a year ago, during one of the wars, in the last century; it may happen in the future. These are sophisticated notions that supposedly mean nothing to an ape. Oh, the things humans think they know! Humans know apes don't understand the difference between today and tomorrow and yesterday. Apes don't know they're going to die. Apes live by instinct. While apes can be, and are, trained to respond to certain stimuli in a certain way, everyone also knows that they don't "think" like humans. Some apes say "Thank god," for not thinking like humans.

Yes, an ape can "say" something to another ape. We have lively conversations with each other about apedom; the state of the ape world; leadership and brilliance; stupidity and evil; humans.

Ape language isn't understood by most humans so there is no point in going into it. It's not like learning Latin, say. When humans know Latin, it's possible for them to read classic works of human literature in their original language, which is far more satisfying than reading works in translation. For all you know, what you're reading may be the translator's creation and not that of the original author. Apes have observed that humans who know Latin, however, seem to know other languages, too. My friend Myrtle, an ape I knew at the University of North Carolina, once told me that it was a pity that ancient Greek was not taught to humans anymore. She told me that her grandmother, Sally, told Myrtle that humans who knew ancient Greek were more interesting than those who did not. Myrtle said that Sally always reminisced morbidly about the past. Sally, Myrtle said, claimed that it was not as good today as it was in the old days. Myrtle thought Sally was a snob. Personally, while I don't mind making observations about others, I don't like to make judgments of the sort that Myrtle made of Sally. Humans, we know, have a notion that every other generation is close, that it takes a grandparent and grandchild to love and understand each other, while parents are considered mean-spirited, ill-comprehending, strict, lenient, etc. Apes don't subscribe to this notion. The generations closest to us—our parents and our children—are the generations we love and revere the most. It is one of the hundreds, even thousands, of areas where apes and humans would find it possible to explore our differences if all of us should ever talk to each other.

It's legitimate to wonder about these names—Myrtle, Sally, and my own, Sasha. These are names given to us by humans. For the sake of making sense of the account that follows, it seems reasonable to assume these and other human names. Otherwise, it would be necessary to teach human readers the whole ape language. This is not a language textbook, however, but an attempt to share with you a personal experience. As I am not by ape-nature reflective, I hope that the facts that I recount will speak for themselves. Your reflection—if you have the sensibilities that lead you toward reflection—will be your own, unguided by a hand that wants to lead.

We came from various places. Some came from their natural habitats in Africa. Most were born in captivity and had only heard about the faraway places from parents and grandparents, who, themselves, sometimes heard about the ancient homelands from old apes who had learned from old apes themselves. I was born in captivity.

We were brought together as part of a scientific experiment. Everyone knows that in an effort to establish finally the links between humans and apes, experiments and studies have gone on for generations. In the United States, where the experiments I participated in were conducted, these links between human and ape are still a pretty tricky thing to bring up in parts of that country where fundamentalist religions are strong. Even apes know and ape-laugh about the famous Scopes trial, and all the foolish declarations made there by nationally—indeed, internationally—prominent people. The Scopes trial is one of the funniest things that ever happened in America, as anyone who has studied that country's history knows. For some crazy reason, lawmakers in Tennessee in 1925 decided that it would be a violation of the law for anybody to teach that "man" was anything other than a divine creation, for that is how the Bible labels "man." Poor John Scopes—he was a teacher—told his students that "man" and apes might be closer than the Tennessee legislature thought possible. Scopes believed in evolution: that "man" had descended from apes. Researchers tell us, now, that nobody descended from anybody, and that "man" and apes have common ancestors. I've also heard that birds are dinosaurs, or their descendants. What does this knowledge do to Bible studies? In any event, when the State of Tennessee decided to prosecute John Scopes for teaching evolution, it hired William Jennings Bryan to represent it. The attorney defending Mr. Scopes was Clarence Darrow, who marveled at the storytelling abilities of the authors of the Bible.

We made up stories about the Scopes trial right from the beginning; they became part of our traditional lore, but we don't repeat them very much anymore because they are condescending. At the risk of offending, however, here's one of the stories. I got it from an old ape named Popeye, who was told it by his father, Walt:

One day during the trial Bryan came down into the hotel dining room to take his supper there. He was alone. As soon as he sat down at a table set for two, he heard a voice behind him.

"Mr. Bryan," the immediately recognizable voice said, "if you are dining alone and are not averse to company, may I join you?"

"Of course," Mr. Bryan said, standing. He motioned to Clarence Darrow that he should take the seat opposite him. Mr. Darrow made a great show of urging Mr. Bryan not to stand, even though he was already standing.

When they had taken their seats, they looked across the table, smiled, but said nothing. A moment passed. And then another. Finally Mr. Darrow said, "This is a quiet little town, isn't it?"

1817

Harper Junior Books

Harper & Row, Publishers

10 East 53rd Street   New York, N.Y. 10022

We take pleasure in sending you this book for review.

TITLE   **FAMILY**

PUB. DATE   April 28, 1976

PRICE   Trade Ed.,$5.95
Harpercrest Lib.Ed.,$5.79

Please send two copies of your review
to Joan Robins, Publicity.

We take pleasure in sending a copy of this book for review.

TITLE **FAMILY**

PUB. DATE April 28, 1976

PRICE Trade Ed., $5.95
Harpercrest Lib.Ed., $5.79

"It is indeed, sir," Mr. Bryan answered.

"What do you do to amuse yourself here, apart from the business associated with the trial, of course?" Mr. Darrow asked.

"Why, I have two close friends in town. I wouldn't want it generally known, but I meet with them regularly, late at night, and we drink together, telling each other stories about the old days. After all, I am many years your senior. If you would care to join me this evening, after eleven o'clock, my friends and I would be pleased to have your company."

Indeed, they met that evening at an arranged place and time. They enjoyed themselves enormously, passing pleasantries, drinking bourbon and branch water, and cementing bonds of friendship that none would forget—Bryan, Darrow, and two apes named Bess and Sugar. When it was time to part, Sugar gave Mr. Darrow a well-worn copy of the King James Version. It is said that thereafter Mr. Darrow valued it more than any other book in his library.

As for the experiment I and the others were associated with, it did not involve language and teaching apes how to recognize human symbols and words. That is the most boring sort of experiment to be a part of, as any ape who has had to endure the experience will tell you. The repetition! It's interminable. Some apes develop human vocabularies of several dozen words; an uncooperative ape, or one who is just bored or hostile or, yes, dumb, may manage only a few words. It all depends on the ape. No, that's not right. It all depends on what's in the ape's mind. An ape who likes the humans who are trying to establish communications between apes and humans will be fairly responsive in certain circumstances. Food makes a difference.

7

Naturally, we are fed. We don't get to pick out our own food because of the living arrangements. The food is brought to us. It's even frequently "used" in the experiments. When we see a banana, a food item that humans have rightly concluded is particularly palatable to apes, we have to develop certain comprehension skills before they'll give us the damn banana. We have to learn to choose between the banana and a hunk of rope in front of us; we sample both and eat the banana. Sometimes they trick us and put only the banana, and they say "ba-nan-a" slowly, distorting the pronunciation of the word so that it is barely recognizable, and thus defeating the purpose of the experiment, it seems to me. However, that's their problem. The trick involved is when they put the rope where the banana should be and they say "ba-nan-a." I won't go into the ethics of such a trick, but dumb apes grab the rope and practically choke to death trying to eat it, and other apes reject the rope. The humans are happy when the rejection takes place. Of course, it's only common sense not to eat the kind of tough rope they provide for these experiments. Then, once the first hurdle is passed by an ape, the people conducting the experiments won't put anything at all in front of us. They'll come to us and say several words. (Simultaneously, they've been "teaching" us words associated with things other than eating.) When they say "ba-nan-a," we're supposed to stick out our hands and gulp, or point to our mouths to show that we know the word is associated with eating and that we want some. So beyond being boring, it's cruelly demeaning. The only positive feature of these language/symbol experiments is that they appear to give work to a lot of humans, especially at the graduate-student level. They

8

always have notebooks or clipboards and they make marks on them every time they do *anything* with an ape.

Occasionally a human involved in these experiments will display a kind of empathy and compassion that touches an ape. There are many stories that we tell each other of deep attachments that grow between apes and humans. My friend Myrtle had a sincere affection for a graduate student named Crossley M. Winkle. Myrtle said that Crossley Winkle didn't seem to give a damn about data retrieval and just liked to play around with Myrtle. They had great times, Myrtle said. They would wrestle a lot, and hit each other—gently, of course. They even danced and kissed and made small talk about a terrific future together. Unfortunately, the human running the experiment didn't think Crossley Winkle was contributing anything to it, so she got kicked out of the program. Myrtle became very uncooperative afterward. She pretended to lose all of her human communication skills. And that is how Myrtle came to join us here at this experiment. Myrtle *does* have most fond recollections of Crossley Winkle, however. She wonders if she's all right, progressing in her career, or totally unproductive as a result of being booted off the language experiment. Myrtle may never forget Crossley Winkle. Because she is an ape, Myrtle will never have any way of finding out what happened to her friend. Apes don't get mail.

A digression, before it slips my mind. Apes are not, after all, elephants, to appropriate an allusion that humans understand because they say it all the time. The digression is about the apes that are from the faraway places that most of us know only through our collective memories, and the lore that generations sit around telling their young about what happened before they got to the zoos, the jungle habitats, the universities and hospitals. The observation about the real natives, the naturals, those straight from the legendary jungles, is that they are different. While all of us understand confinement, and that you can move only so far when there are walls, locked doors, bars over windows and the like, the apes from abroad (oh, that is a strange notion!) don't understand these limitations at all. As a consequence, they're forever bumping into things. They are unruly companions until they learn and adapt to the limitations of confinement.

Another observation about the naturals is that they look different from the rest of us. They are invariably stronger. This is logical, given their background. They have had to use parts of their bodies in ways that we captives never do. I try to befriend the naturals. I make the friendship gestures. But the naturals have fears related to new associations. After the fears go away, I get a particular pleasure in feeling the long line of bone joints that stretch from their necks down their backs. In a natural ape, this line of joints is magnificent. It's different in us captives. Our joints, in this area, are more like those of humans. While they have a function, and are used appropriately, there is no magnificence, no strength, no real sense of purpose to these joints that, for the naturals, is so evident. It makes a captive ape wonder about ancestors, and what being an ape really is.

Now we come to their natures. They *are* different. For all their physical strength and magnificence, they are innocent of the world they have unfortunately found themselves thrust into. Captive apes sometimes refer to the naturals as jungle bumpkins. I've never joined in with the captives who get a lot of laughs when a natural bumps into

10

a wall, or tumbles and falls climbing toward a sky that is only a ceiling, or who gets hurt in other ways because captivity is so new. They *seem* fierce, and, in fact, the fury in some never disappears. As for others, they learn their new place, and they take on new friends.

Ape language. As between the captives and the naturals, there are few similarities. The naturals must retrogress (for ape language has continued to grow "abroad") to use the language of the captives. It is as though English-speaking humans had suddenly to speak their language as it was spoken two, three or four centuries ago, by Samuel Johnson or by Ben Jonson.

The experiment that brought twenty-three of us apes together took place at a state university in the eastern part of the United States. I could name the state—one of the original thirteen, to narrow it considerably—but there is no point in dishonoring its past by identifying it with its present inglorious activities. There is a theory among futurists—people who try to identify what life will be like in the next generation, a hundred years from now, five hundred, etc.—that it will be possible to manipulate bodies. These futurists subscribe to the notion, for example, that humans might one day be "put together," composed of parts taken from here and there that, in combination, will make up a functioning human. It may be possible, they think, that certain malfunctioning parts, or parts otherwise missing, can be manufactured and installed in humans. It's conceivable that a whole human could be created in this way. These are serious thoughts entertained by serious speculators. The humans who would emerge at some future time would be just like today's humans, only perfect. If, before these perfect humans materialize, there is a time when only part of the human is real, and part created by other humans, there will be a kind of class warfare between those most nearly or even totally created by other humans and those created by the natural process of copulation, leading to birth and life, and ending in death. The speculation among the futurists is that the more created a human being is, the more nearly perfect will that human be. It will follow that there will be fewer and fewer natural, and consequently imperfect, humans, and that at some time in the very distant future, there won't be a need for humans created in the natural way. Such persons will, therefore, be suppressed. The world will be in the control of the now-perfect humans who have made the decision to suppress the other humans. There won't be new humans added unless they are needed. If, subsequently, there are too many, the excess numbers can be dis-assembled and their parts held in reserve until once again needed. These future humans would not be robots, mind you. They would be humans. Robots are associated with comic books, horror movies and science-fiction stories. Definitely not robots. Humans.

I heard all these things from the scientists who brought us twenty-three apes together. They didn't tell me, or us, directly, of course. I overheard what they said. It was their habit to sit around talking, always drinking coffee—coffee, coffee, coffee—for hours in our quarters. I was one of the first to come to the university. I had been used at one of the boring language experiments at another university several months before, and that university didn't know what to do with me and the three other apes when their experiments were over. Excess baggage. Sam and Ginger, two of the apes, were given to a nearby zoo. Ginny, the

12

third, had a heart attack and died. It was sudden, induced I am sure by the prospect of having to live and entertain in a zoo. She was a good ape, and it broke me up to see her go. I thought I was lucky to get to go to yet another university laboratory. I had already gone through five language experiments. I could have written a thesaurus if anyone had taken the trouble to look into my background. Nobody ever did, however, so I always played along with the graduate students with their notebooks, clipboards and starched white jackets.

I could name all twenty-three apes that were brought together for the futuristic experiments, but I will not do that. I have to mention Myrtle from the University of North Carolina, however, becouse it was an absolute joy to see her again. She was a first-class ape. She was gabby, but very interesting; she never gossiped, but she was always up on the news; we shared an admiration for Thomas Wolfe as a result of everything we heard about him at UNC, and once got an understanding student to read us the whole of *Look Homeward, Angel* and *Of Time and the River*, and long passages from other works. Myrtle and I knew that Wolfe was passé, but we had many ape-talks and ape-cries over those Wolfe books, you can be sure. Myrtle was one ape everyone enjoyed having around. When she came to the new place, the scientists there thought Myrtle and I would be lovers right away. But it wasn't that way with us. We were *friends*. Humans don't understand friendship between male and female.

Of the twenty-three apes in the new experiment, eighteen were captives. Most were quite young, four of them only about two or three years old. They had been separated from their mothers and were totally confused. When they arrived it was a full-time job for the rest of us just to keep track of them. Lollipop was the worst. She wouldn't believe one of us was not her mother, and kept jumping from ape to ape twenty-four hours a day. When the naturals came Lollipop rushed at them with such abandon that I feared for her life. Naturals don't tolerate many of the ways of captives. I have observed it of them in the past that their young, when they are accompanied by their young, behave deferentially toward the elders. This must be the jungle way. I thought the naturals might interpret Lollipop's onslaught as an attack and might kill her on the spot and without misgivings, as well. Even captives know of "the law of the jungle," "survival of the fittest," and all the other stuff humans believe about life in the faraway lands. Fortunately for Lollipop, the naturals were so filled with tranquilizing drugs given them to keep them calm on their long journey that they only stared at her blankly, huddled together—at least four of them did— and slept soundly for several hours. The fifth natural, Moses, the most powerful and forbidding ape I have ever seen, kept apart from the others, though he, too, fell asleep immediately. The rest of us stood around the naturals, staring at them, eager to wake them up and try to under-stand their stories about their homelands, to see if they jibed with all the stuff we had heard from others. Of course, it would be many weeks, perhaps months, until they could retrogress in their ape-language skills to a point where there could be meaningful communication among us. We would have to be patient.

I was to learn later that the four naturals who huddled together that first day, and who continued afterward to stay as close together as they could, were from the same place and were, in fact, related. There were a brother and

14

sister, a nephew, and their second cousin whom they hardly knew before. In their country she had visited her own family on ceremonial occasions only. Well, times had certainly changed for Hortense, the name the humans gave her. In the weeks that followed she couldn't have been more solicitous and kindly toward her family, and they warmed to her, too. Apes don't carry grudges.

As for Moses, he had come from another place entirely. More of that later. It was such an interesting thing for us captives to sit gathered around the naturals. I could sense every ape's imagination at work as we stared at these hulks in our midst, and especially at Moses. I stayed as close to him as I dared stay. Lollipop kept trying to pounce on the new arrivals, so I took charge of her. I drew her to me. "Lollipop," I said as soothingly as I could, "put your arms around me. Sasha will hold you close and comfort you. Sasha will be your momma for a few hours. Would you like that, Lollipop?"

The others thought the idea of my being Lollipop's mother was so funny that they had some wonderful ape-laughs. Not Lollipop. She grabbed hold of me. The others stopped ape-laughing when they saw that for the first time in days Lollipop slept. I inched even closer to Moses. He smelled wonderful, and I knew that in due course the smell of his homeland that he brought with him would disappear from him entirely. I had seen it happen with other apes, and Moses would be no exception.

I had never before been associated with an experiment where the ape arrangements were so casual. It is customary that captives and naturals are kept apart for some time, until the naturals have a chance to adapt to their new place. Not so on this experiment. It is customary that no more than four, or five at the most, apes share quarters, separated from the others by bars, or cages. Not so on this experiment. It is customary that very young apes taken from their mothers are not immediately housed with mature apes. Not so on this experiment. There all of us were, all twenty-three, in a big room that had been a basketball court only two years before, when a multi-millionaire alumnus had given the university a new and grander basketball court that was named for him. The place was filled with the odor of eight thousand basketball games. That odor had not gone away, even after two years. The apes would soon take care of that.

The scientists had rigged up several things designed for our comfort. There were fake trees with reinforced limbs; metal poles arranged in such a way that we would enjoy scampering about on, in and through them; metal rings hung on ropes attached to the ceiling; and a cave-like construction that would allow us dark and privacy if we felt like being alone or apart.

During the first weeks there was nothing to do. As I was among the first to arrive, and overheard the humans discussing their theories, I deduced that we apes were to be associated with these futuristic notions. As pleased as I was that the experiments did not involve communications, I had an uncomfortable feeling, like a chill, about the whole business. As the apes arrived, I could see that most were on the young side, and when the four infants came on one day I had a bad premonition. When Myrtle came, there was first the joy of seeing my old friend and, second, the chance to discuss my premonition with some-one I trusted and whose counsel I valued.

I told her the whole business—about the human conversations overheard, about their theories of body manipulation and about the very great numbers of apes being accumulated for the experiment.

"Sasha," Myrtle said, "I can't believe there is any relation between these fantastic theories and their bringing together so many apes."

"But it stands to reason," I insisted. "It's all they talk about. They sit here at the table in the middle of this stinking gymnasium, patting us on the head when we lumber up to them, and what they're doing is planning to rip us apart and put us together again in other combinations."

"You're crazy, Sasha!"

"I'm not crazy."

"I've lived through many experiments in my day, and so have you. None of them ever involved anything such as you're describing. I don't believe humans would do the things you're saying. It's simply inape."

"Times have changed, Myrtle," I said. "They want more. They're going to get more. Technological and scientific advancement is the name of the game."

"You've picked up human slang," Myrtle said, apelaughing.

I had to ape-laugh, too. "That could be," I said. "But my instincts are customarily right. Don't you think so?"

"Yes," Myrtle said. "But in this case . . . I don't know."

"Watch what happens."

The naturals came and for several days I did not return to this subject with Myrtle. All of us captives spent our time trying to get to know the naturals, trying to make them retrogress so that we could have good visits. Hortense and her family were agreeable about the whole thing. In

17

just a few days they began to pick up the simple ape language of an earlier day that we speak. They were eager to unlearn all that the generations of life in a faraway land had taught them. They were a lot of fun, even though the nephew in the group—he got the name Otto—fantasized a great deal. He was only about four-and-a-half and he said that he had the achievements that even a twenty-year-old ape would be immodest to claim.

"He's wonderful," Hortense let us know. I think she was trying to make up for all the time she had been hoity-toity in their homeland. She hardly knew Otto.

Moses kept himself apart from Hortense and her newly discovered family, and from us captives as well. He moved around the gymnasium awkwardly. Once he came toward the table in the middle of the floor. Two of the scientists were sitting there. They became tense as Moses approached the table.

"Hello, Moses," the human said, smiling. What a particularly dumb thing for the human to do—smile. Any sensible human who knows apes knows a human smile means the human is filled with fear.

Moses stopped moving toward the table. The scientist put out her hand; she seemed to want to shake his hand. Moses stared at her briefly. He continued walking toward the table. He pushed it aside. The scientists hurried out of the gymnasium. An ape ape-laughed but was quieted by other apes in a half-second.

Moses often went into the fake cave made for us and slept. No other ape went inside when he was there. No ape made a friendly gesture to Moses. He was too formidable, too great in strength, for us to risk a rebuff.

When it came time for us to be fed, we could see that Moses got more food than the rest of us. It was never

18

enough, however, so Moses would grab and eat food meant for other apes. No ape went without food, however, for we saw to it that an ape robbed by Moses would get small portions from several other apes' meals. One day Lollipop was robbed by Moses and she made a fuss. She tried to get her food back, but Moses smacked her hard. Poor Lollipop. She came to me, crying. I and several others gave her more food than she'd ever had before, so she was happy. But I think she got tough that day.

Sometimes, when Moses was awake and roaming around the gymnasium, he would sit for many minutes, even an hour on several occasions, wide-awake, staring blankly at nothing. I would try to disengage myself from whatever I was doing on those occasions. I would sit, too, or hang on one of the fake tree limbs, to look at Moses. If he knew I was looking at him, he never acknowledged it. I could not get as close to him then as I had been on his first night at the gymnasium, and I missed the smell of his homeland that he had brought with him. Sometimes, as he passed nearby, I would try to smell him but it was not as it had been on that first night.

The examinations began. I was the third ape to be examined. The humans came one morning and led me by the hand downstairs in the gymnasium. The old locker area had been rigged up as an office. There were machines and instruments everywhere. Beyond, a great metal table stood in the middle of what had been the shower room. I shuddered when I saw it. It was right next to a big floor drain. I got the image of some of my parts being tossed into that drain.

I got strapped to the metal table. They spent three

19

hours on me that day, and shorter periods on other days. Various instruments were wheeled over to the table and hooked on to one part or another of me. They looked inside me with other instruments, and took samples of this and that from me. If I had mastered human language it would be possible to be more explicit about these examinations, but I have not. Besides, the humans seldom spoke whole sentences, but only isolated words and numbers. The combinations were dizzying after a while so I gave up trying to figure out the whole business. I suppose that if I were a human they would have explained each thing they did to me. They didn't know how interested I was.

In about three weeks all of the apes except Moses had had a series of examinations. When it was time to examine Moses, each time the humans came near him he got furious. That is the way with a male ape. A female ape is more cunning. She would have let them approach closely and then clobbered the humans. So from day to day they kept putting off his examinations.

"The only way to get him down there is to tranquilize him," one of the scientists said.

They had numerous discussions about that possibility. Two days after all of the other apes had finished with the examinations, one of the humans brought in a dart gun and they shot Moses from a distance. Moses grabbed the dart from his buttocks and threw it toward the humans. He made a terrifying noise, too. They shot him again, and this time Moses couldn't get out the dart so easily. He tried, but in less than a minute he collapsed onto the gymnasium floor. All of us were frightened; some thought the humans had killed Moses. I explained to the most scared that Moses was put to sleep only so he could be examined.

They did this for three days with Moses, who finally got so dopey that they had to stop. Besides, at least half, if not more than half, of their tests would have been wasted on a drugged subject. They could hardly determine how Moses functioned if they made him non-functioning. The humans had a lot of discussion about that, of course.

Moses! He gave them one hell of a time. For when they'd get him to sleep, they had to lug him down to the shower room. I'll bet more than one of them got a hernia. Ha!

Two days passed. A third. And yet a fourth.

"Do you think that's all?" Myrtle asked me.

"No," I said.

On the fifth day, eight new humans joined the scientists who had been with us until then. Five of the eight were quite old, and three were perhaps in their late twenties. You can tell humans' ages by the degree of drowsiness that surrounds them and by the way they stand. Each human has a drowsy degree, and apes can recognize it immediately, give or take ten percentage points. A human with a 40% drowsy degree is a forty-year-old human; 15%, fifteen years old; 80%, eighty years old. It's easy to figure out the degree once an ape gets the hang of it, and each of us does. Zoo apes tell me that that's practically all they do in zoos: figure out the drowsy degrees of all the people who come to look at them.

The standing business is more subtle, and many apes never get onto that. Apes have a keen eye for backbones, and how a human stands depends on the health of the backbone, which deteriorates with age. Some apes say that is pure theory, and a crackpot one at that. Even if it's an old ape's tale, I believe it. Apes always have to re-examine their theories and notions, of course, but we have that ability I'm glad to say. Sometimes a human with a 28% drowsy degree will carry a stick, or even sit in a metal chair with wheels. What matters is the drowsy degree in determining that person's age; we disregard the standing factor. Incidentally, humans with sticks and who sit on metal chairs look at apes differently than free-standing humans. Every ape makes that comment, so I take it to be a universal truth.

The eight new humans strolled about the gymnasium, looking. As they came to each of us, one of the scientists would rattle off comments about each ape. They were clearly reporting on the examinations that had been made. Again, the talk was so rapid and the language so un-familiar that I couldn't make out what most of it meant. The new humans were silent for the most part. They nodded a lot. The three youngest ones, in particular, made a lot of notes.

Moses was, as usual, apart from the others. He was sitting in a far corner of the gymnasium, and the scientists and the newcomers had a long walk before they got near him. He ignored them. A scientist began to rattle off Moses' report.

"The problem with the remarks on Moses," the scientist said, "is that he had to be under total sedation for all the tests."

"Why?" asked one of the new humans.

"He is a wild beast in the exact sense of the word *wild*. He can't be approached."

"You mean he's not used to confinement?"

"That's correct, ma'am. He's straight from the jungle."

"Don't you think it's dangerous, to him and the others, to have him living with the other apes?"

"He doesn't have anything to do with the others, ma'am. Nor do they have anything to do with him."

"Poor fella," the woman said. She walked close to Moses. She was one of those humans who use a stick; she had a 70% drowsy degree. Possibly the stick made the approach to Moses agreeable to him. She reached out to him and rubbed the back of his head for several minutes. "Poor fella," she kept saying over and over. Moses reached out to the woman and rubbed the back of her head, too.

The next day everything was quiet. There were no visitors and fewer scientists than usual. We got our meals all right. Most of the apes didn't notice anything unusual about the day.

"I think they're going to start soon," I said to Myrtle.

"Sasha, you're making me a nervous wreck with all your apprehensions. Now, stop it."

"I can feel it," I said.

As the day passed and nighttime came, it wasn't a feeling anymore. I knew something was up. I couldn't sleep that night. I lumbered around the gymnasium all night. I found myself sitting near Moses. Moses was awake, too. He had great black eyes, bigger than any I'd ever seen in an ape before. The moon was full that night and it shone on Moses' big eyes. He was staring directly at me. I nodded. He kept staring, not unfriendly, but not friendly either. All the other apes were sleeping. After a few moments I moved closer to Moses. He didn't move away, so I moved even closer.

"Moses," I said. "That's what they call you, 'Moses.'"

Moses kept staring at me.

"Moses is an important figure in their great books, so they no doubt meant it as a compliment when they gave you the name Moses."

Moses stared.

"They call me 'Sasha.' My name is Sasha."

It was as it had been.

"It's crazy for me to go on talking this ridiculous ape language to you. I know your language is far more developed than ours. But, you see, I was born in San Diego, California. There is no way for us captives to keep up with your language. Perhaps you can teach me some words, and we can make ape-talk now and then. I would like that, Moses."

I thought I would make the friendship gesture, but I was fearful that he would reject it. It was, I decided, too soon to make the friendship gesture.

"I can also teach you our language. You will know many of the words already. Naturals still use them. Sometimes their meaning has changed, and I can teach you the new meanings." I ape-laughed. "I mean the old meanings, of course."

I pointed to myself. "Sasha," I said. I pointed to him. "Moses," I said. I repeated it.

Then I noticed that Moses had closed his eyes and was making deep sleep noises.

Otto, the young natural, was the first to be led away. He had by now learned our language extremely well, so perhaps certain of the things he had previously bragged about were true. Perhaps the humans had discovered that Otto was an especially superior ape. He ape-beamed with delight when it was clear that he would be taken away first.

When I say "taken away," it's not that they spirited him off. Early in the morning, after we had been fed, four scientists took Otto aside. They looked him over thoroughly. They had various harmless instruments that they used for this purpose. The instruments were connected to small machines; one of them was connected to a scientist's ears and was placed on Otto's chest. Otto thought it was the tickle game, so he tickled the scientist back. Otto ape-laughed and all the scientists human-laughed. Most of the rest of us apes ape-laughed, too. Otto and the scientist played the tickle game for several minutes. I glanced at Myrtle, who looked petulant. The tickle game is her absolute favorite, and I knew that she envied Otto's getting to play it in front of all of us. Myrtle is *not* small-minded. I don't want to give that impression. She enjoys her pleasures and wants to indulge in them whenever she can.

After spending close to an hour examining Otto in this way, the four scientists left and two others came. Their examination, if that's what it was, was brisk. They had some objects with them. One of them stood near Otto, and the other some distance from him. The one who stood at a distance had the objects. First he threw a basketball (how appropriate!) to Otto, who caught it and threw it back. The second time the basketball was thrown to Otto, he missed it, but went after it and threw it back. The next object was a banana. Otto caught it, peeled it immediately and swallowed it in three gulps. He ape-laughed as he threw the peelings back at the scientist, who human-laughed. Next came a smaller ball, maybe a tennis ball. Otto had a hard time catching such a little ball, but by the fourth throw he caught it properly and threw it back.

"Good boy," the scientist closest to Otto said, as he patted Otto on the back. The scientists left.

Otto pranced around the gymnasium, followed closely by Hortense. Hortense kept saying, "Oh, Otto, you're wonderful," to him. And to all of us, "Aren't his reflexes magnificent? Isn't Otto wonderful?" It was a sickening display of self-congratulation; and I don't mean that to be a judgment, but an observation. It was *that* obvious. Finally Otto came to rest, and nine apes gathered close to him. Hortense, of course, and his aunt and uncle; and six captives of the sort who get deeply impressed with others, natural followers. Nice apes, of course, but without personalities of their own, the sort of apes whose names it is difficult to remember. Otto didn't have anything to say. He just sat there, as self-designated heroes do, exuding false modesty.

Eventually several scientists came back.

"Otto," one of them called out.

Otto got up and moved toward the scientists, who admired Otto's immediate response to the call. One of the scientists took Otto's hand in his own. As they turned to leave the gymnasium, Otto glanced back at all of us and, ape-beaming, waved.

After Otto left, there was a near-festive feeling about the gymnasium. Most of the apes began to chat vigorously with each other. Everyone was speculating about where Otto had gone and what would happen to him. Several told Hortense and Otto's aunt and uncle that they must be proud and excited. They said they were. It became quite gay. One of the captive apes who had spent time

26

in *both* a zoo and a circus (the only circus ape I've ever met), and who was quite an entertainer, sang ape-songs that encouraged dancing and tumbling; and before long it was like one of the parties apes have together on July 14, the date captive apes throughout the world have selected as the beginning of the ape year. Humans in France observe Bastille Day on that date, too. Funny, isn't it?

"Don't be such a stick-in-the-dirt," Myrtle said to me when I did not join in the festivities.

"Mud," I said.

"What?"

"If you're going to appropriate human slang, do it correctly," I said. "It's 'stick-in-the-mud,' not 'dirt.'"

"Oh, what difference does it make? Anyway, let's wrestle together. Everyone is having a lot of fun, except you and him," Myrtle said, pointing to Moses.

I looked at Moses, sitting as usual removed from the others and in a far corner of the gymnasium. He looked at me, too. He nodded.

"No thanks, Myrt," I said.

"Sasha, don't call me 'Myrt'! You know I hate it." Myrtle gave me a playful poke, and somersaulted away from me to seek jollier companions.

I looked again at Moses. Again he nodded, and so did I.

Evening came. They brought food. The merrymakers had exhausted themselves long ago, and by late in the day there had been some deep sleeping. In fact, more than half the apes had to be waked up when the food came. The scientists had not been with us much during the day. Occasionally one looked in for a few minutes. The apes calmed themselves but as soon as the human left, the roistering began again. So when they brought the food in the evening it was a surprise to the humans to find so many of the apes asleep.

"They're usually pouncing on us when we come," a human said.

"It's strange, isn't it?" said another.

In a few moments it was the usual scramble, however, for the activities of the day had left most of the apes hungrier than usual. Even so, most ate in silence.

"They're acting strangely," the human who had made the observation before said again.

Two more humans came. They walked around the gymnasium, greeting us all by name. They smiled and stroked most of us. Myrtle was determined to get in some tickling, so she tickled one of the humans, who tickled her back. The uneasy edge that seemed to be hanging over both apes and humans disappeared as everyone watched Myrtle and the human tickle. There were little ape-laughs and little human-laughs.

"I guess everything's all right," the human who had been concerned about the strangeness said.

One of the customs of apes is to make a prayer for the provider of our food after it has been eaten. We have heard that some humans make a prayer for the provider before the food is eaten, and that custom seems strange to us, indeed. What if the food is no good? Or what if it makes the humans sick? It seems reckless to apes that humans thank the provider in advance. The provider may be pulling a fast one, to use human slang yet again, and there may be nothing to be thankful for.

28

The prayers apes make for the providers depend greatly on the quality of the food provided. If the food is especially good and plentiful as well, it is appropriate that the prayer be lengthy, so as to show proper appreciation. Sometimes, all that apes get is garbage left over from humans' tables. Most of such food is indigestible and also gives apes gas pains. But it's eaten if that's the only food provided. On such occasions, apes agree, it is not appropriate to make a prayer for the provider.

This good custom is part of an ape's heritage. Naturals understand it immediately, for it began in our ancestral jungles, though it's not so formal a ritual in the homelands. It is more an ordinary thing there; lesser apes, in their maturity, express gratitude to the greater apes on whom they must rely. So when naturals come together with captives, it is a quite usual thing to the naturals that the prayer for the provider be made. The prayer is sometimes our first ape contact that makes sense to naturals, whose adjustments are severe. There are problems with naturals like Moses, for example, for he is one ape whose manner suggests that he was more often the thanked than the thanker. Such apes find it impossible to join in with the prayers for the provider. It is understood among captives that an ape should pray only if the gratitude is felt. So no ape is forced to join in the ritual.

After each meal, where there is a community of apes, our custom is that each ape, in turn, gets a chance to make the prayer. Some apes are more eloquent than others. Some apes are still hungry. Some are long-winded. Some are shy and express themselves modestly; it is not unusual for a shy ape to say "Thank you for the meal," and nothing more. When the prayer is over, the maker says "Aape," and all the apes say "Aape," which is the signal for us to return to our ordinary pursuits. No ape is forced to make the prayer, and other apes don't think anything of it if the ape whose turn it is to lead passes on that opportunity to the ape whose turn follows next.

On this particular evening, it was Dylys' turn to make the prayer. She was about nine or ten years old, and when her times to lead had come before, she had passed. In fact, I'd never heard Dylys say an ape-word. She was one shy ape. I expected her to pass again. Solomon, recently at the University of Oklahoma, followed Dylys on the roster. Solomon was a good-hearted old ape, but he surely did like the sound of his own ape-voice. It was his habit to begin everything he said with, "It's not for nothing that I have the name Solomon." Then he would go on and on. Making the prayer was a big event for Solomon. He looked shocked when Dylys indicated that this evening she would make the prayer. That meant Solomon would make the prayer in the morning, and, by custom, morning prayers are brief.

"I've never made the prayer before," Dylys began. "So if I don't do it well, please forgive me."

The apes ape-smiled encouragingly. Solomon did, too.

"The food the humans brought tonight was good. It's always good here. In fact, I don't think I've ever had better food. So I suppose I'm grateful. It seems only right to be grateful." She paused. Everyone thought she'd say "Aape." But she didn't say it. A few apes got restless. "I have a strange feeling," Dylys continued. "While the food is good, I'm not sure about the humans." She paused again. "Aape," she said.

"Aape," we answered.

Dylys' prayer wasn't ceremonial in the way Solomon's

were. None of the apes went about their usual nighttime frolics. There was stirring in the gymnasium. Most of the apes turned away from Dylys. Some stared at her.

After several minutes, the rumblings began. First, Hortense said it: "Where's Otto?" She said it quietly the first time, but when she said it a second and third time she wasn't quiet at all. The apes began to make alarm sounds. To humans, they sound like screeches and seem to be uncontrolled. Not so to apes. "Otto," apes began shouting, "where is he?"

The roar was deafening. Several humans came. The apes were sprinting around. "Otto, where is he?" they kept repeating. The humans backed away.

It was an hour before the apes became calm again.

"Damnedest thing," a human said. "What came over these critters?"

When quiet came, I went to Dylys. I made the friendship gesture, and she made it back. I took her hand and led her to Moses, who had of course remained apart from the general hysteria. Dylys and I sat in front of Moses for many minutes. She made the friendship gesture to him at last; he made it back. I made the friendship gesture to him; he made it back.

No ape slept that night. Some dozed for a few moments, but would become alert at the slightest noise. And there was a lot of noise. Apes kept shuffling around the gymnasium. By the time midway between dark and daylight, four humans had come to the gymnasium. The humans had never before been with us during the sleeping time, and their presence added to the unrest. It was a terrible night. The apes did not calm themselves until the sky began to get light outside. Then several went into deep sleep. Not all, by any means.

When it came time for the morning food, it was eaten in a most desultory manner. Solomon's prayer that followed was positively cryptic. It was easy to observe that the humans were puzzled.

Within an hour the four scientists who had examined Otto on the previous day came with the same instruments and machines they had brought before. There was a horrible commotion among the apes. The scientists were baffled. As they walked around the gymnasium, each ape they approached moved away. They called us by our names. When we heard our names we wondered if it was because they had selected us for the examination.

One of the scientists took Walnut, an infant who had come to the gymnasium at the same time Lollipop came. With the exception of Lollipop, the infants had not been deeply involved with the hours of unrest that had followed Dylys' prayer of the night before. For the infants, who squirmed a lot anyway, it had seemed only that the older apes were acting more naturally—that is, like infants—than usual. They hardly understood ape language and had few apprehensions about anything.

The scientists began their examination of Walnut, but the little ape was so squirmish that they abandoned the examination.

"He's under three years old, I'd guess," one of the humans said. "The other one is considerably more developed."

Hortense scampered up to the human who had just spoken. She did not yet understand the human language, so she could not have known that the human was alluding to Otto.

32

"Where's Otto?" she shrieked at the human. "Where's Otto? Where is he?"

The human moved away from Hortense, but she kept after him. "Where's Otto? Where's Otto?" She would not stop shrieking. There was no way to know if the human understood her. Humans are known by apes to be devious on occasion. There are many tales of human deviousness that apes recount to each other.

Some captive apes have had long conversations with at least one human. Some apes have had long and repeated talks with uncounted numbers of humans. I have cited an example already. You will remember that the reason Myrtle found herself a part of this experiment grew out of the cessation of her merriment and conversations with the graduate student Crossley Winkle. When Crossley Winkle got booted off the project that brought her together with Myrtle, Myrtle became uncooperative.

In the old days it was the common belief among apes that talk between humans and apes could take place only in circumstances where trust and true communion prevailed. There is a barrier that some humans and some apes can cross. The barrier is not often crossed, however. When this event takes place it is understood that it will be kept a secret from others, at least while the relationship itself is going on. The reasons for the secrecy are that if others knew of the talks, they would listen in; if others knew, they would plant questions and arrange situations that would introduce third, fourth and even more interests in what is an essentially private and personal relationship; and that if others knew, there would be an ever-present possibility for treachery on the part of third parties. Among apes, the rule is that *after* the talks have ceased, it is expected that apes will tell other apes everything they have talked about with and learned from humans. Many hours are passed among apes in this way; apes have the fondest memories of many humans with whom they have talked. And all apes have a chance to grow in intelligence and wisdom when the talks are recounted to them. The rule appears to be quite different among humans. When the talks are finished, humans tell us, there is a danger in admitting that they have taken place. When humans insist to other humans that there have been talks, they are evidently tranquilized with a dart shotgun until they admit the talks did not take place. And if they still insist there were talks, these humans are placed in institutions for mentally unbalanced humans, where they are studied just as apes are always the subject of studies. In such institutions, some humans tell us, there is frequently no other creature—human, ape, anyone—to talk to, so the human ceases to talk altogether, or talks in such a way that other humans do not understand what is being said. Some humans speculate that other humans institutionalized in this way talk in ape language; they regret that there are not more humans who have this language facility. It would be a good thing if humans would continually re-examine the subjects for which academic credit might be given.

There have been instances in the past few years, apes believe, when the bonds of secrecy, so necessary to sustain the conversations while they are in full bloom, have been broken by humans. There is, in fact, a justifiably famous case that all apes shudder to think of—the famous talks that took place between an ape named Hubert and a scientist named April Showers. Cursed with a name that everyone made fun of throughout her life, she developed a mean and devious disposition at about the age of three. But April Showers was a brilliant scientist, and linguist as well, and her studies of primates are acknowledged to be the most outstanding published so far. Still, when she is introduced—"I'd like you to meet Dr. April Showers"—other humans invariably burst into human-laughter. She advanced into middle and then old age, raging at parents who had cursed her life with a name that people mocked, and too proud to change that name, for in primate-studies circles it inspired awe and respect. Gripped by her inner furies, she found the ape Hubert, with whom she had close and intimate talks. She learned behavior secrets that other humans knew because of *their* intimate talks with *their* apes but would never reveal because of the mutual trust between ape and human that exists in these circumstances. She noted each of the secrets Hubert revealed to her. Without ever revealing her source, she turned all of the revelations into academic jargon, published her findings and found her reputation even more enhanced. It was an ultimate betrayal of trust. It is traditional among apes, now, to utter curses directed toward her when the month of April arrives each year and whenever it rains.

But this is a digression, prompted by Hortense's insistent shrieks about Otto, directed to the human who had remarked on Walnut's age.

"Calm down, there, Hortense," this same human said to her. "Quit screaming at me, will you?"

"Seems pretty lively and alert, doesn't she?" another human observed.

"Sure does."

"Let's go with her."

"All right."

Two humans took hold of Hortense's hands. "Where's

Otto?" she continued to shriek. They led her through the door and downstairs. Other humans gathered together the machines and instruments they had brought with them and followed.

The time had come for me to speak to the apes. It was true that other apes might have had the same conclusions I had, for I was not the first to join the experiment. Others had heard the talk made by the scientists in the days before the apes arrived in substantial numbers, but I did not know those apes well enough, then, to ask them about their knowledge of languages. It was enough that we passed our idle hours in ape-talk, each telling something, but holding back something, too, that might be revealed as our various relationships developed. There is nothing more tedious than an ape who tells all on the first meeting. There is no place to go in an ape relationship afterward.

As the apes began to arrive at the gymnasium in substantial numbers, the scientists' rambling discourses about the future stopped. The humans became more interested in the qualities of each of the new apes than in their own mad theories. So the responsibility was mine.

"I still can't believe that what you're saying can be true," Myrtle said, after I revealed to her that I must tell the others what I had already told her. "Besides, the apes are edgy enough already. There could be a panic. What would that accomplish?"

"I have a responsibility to apes."

"Have it your own way," Myrtle said. "If you ask me, they're just trying to teach Otto and Hortense how to play basketball. You saw that nonsense yesterday, with the human and all those ball throws between him and Otto.

They're probably going to teach us all, and send us on a cross-country promotional tour for some good-sports-make-good-citizens thing the government is interested in. This is a gimmicky world, Sasha, and you've got to stop seeing horrors everywhere."

"I have a responsibility to apes," I said again.

"Have it your way. Personally, I'd rather wrestle. Wanna?"

"No."

I lumbered off to a corner to think matters out. Myrtle had a quick and easy way of speaking, but she was one wise ape and I would never dismiss anything she said simply because she said it without seeming to think deeply beforehand. Apes assess other apes, and I would always respect anything Myrtle said.

I was sitting alone with my thoughts. Except I turned and discovered I was not alone. Moses had come close to me and sat nearby.

"Moses," I said, "I have a big problem. Do you understand?"

Moses stared at me. He gave no sign that he understood or that he did not understand.

"I know what will happen to us here. Of all the apes, I am the only one who has this knowledge, except for Myrtle, who calls me an alarmist. Do you understand?"

As before, Moses gave no response.

"What should I do, Moses?"

Moses made the friendship gesture.

"Apes," I began, "I am not an orator. I am a common ape, like you. I say what I think. I have been a captive for all of my life, but this does not mean that I am less

37

an ape than any other. I have lived most of my life as a subject for research. Some apes think that research apes consider themselves superior to other apes, but that is because they may not have been associated with research projects before. Apes are apes, wherever they may be. Most are kind; some are not. Most are bright and lively; some are not. Most are generous; some are selfish. Apes are apes. And I am an ape.

"So know that I am speaking ape to ape when I tell you what I must tell you."

There was a stirring. Myrtle closed her eyes. She was crying.

"The humans here have a plan. It is a heavy plan. It is about their future.

"They think that one day in their future, humans will be able to be made up of parts that other humans will put together. The humans think that in the future, copulation will not be a factor associated with creating lives. They think they will be able to assemble themselves and take themselves apart according to their needs.

"We—you and I—will help them, they think."

A great stirring then occurred.

"I want no part of this experiment," I said.

A shrieking began, and grew louder and louder. Humans in great numbers came to the gymnasium. Apes did the unspeakably rude thing they sometimes do when they want to show their contempt for humans. The humans hate it, to be hit with what we throw. It is a dirty and brutish act, but not an inappropriate one when the occasion warrants. The apes felt this to be an appropriate occasion. The humans left in haste. We apes were left alone.

"What next, Sasha?" one of the apes said.

"We must leave this place," I said.

A plan was made. Three committees were formed. One was the intelligence committee, assigned to observe the security precautions the humans had made for us, and to plan when would be the best time to leave.

"It's not for nothing that my name is Solomon," that garrulous old ape said in insisting that he lead the intelligence committee. It was as good a choice as any. To work with him, he selected two crafty captives with a reputation as spies anyway; Otto's uncle, because of his arms that could go exploring on their own—they were so particularly long; and Lollipop, because of her impulsive nature and natural charm that could be useful if any humans were to discover the intelligence committee in forbidden places. Part of this committee's assignment was to steal the necessary keys.

I headed the military affairs committee that would plan the actual leaving and be responsible for combat and defense once we were out. Moses was my deputy, though I'm sure he did not understand his assignment. His size and strength dictated his role, however. Four other tough apes got on this committee, too.

Myrtle was to head the supply committee, charged with stealing food and other necessaries. Apes not on the other two committees were assigned to Myrtle's committee.

Apart from feeding us for the next three days, the humans left us to ourselves, so alarmed had they been with the onslaught against them after my address to the apes. The committees did their work well. By the end of the first day, Solomon's committee had lifted the keys from the pockets of one of the humans; while most of the keys proved useless, one was for the door leading to the floor below and another opened a door that led to the university grounds outside the gymnasium. The crafty ape inappropriately named Gentle did the actual lifting of the keys. Everyone congratulated her, commenting all the while that it was pleasingly stupid of the humans that so many of them had so many vital keys. Each human had several.

My committee made its plans, and Myrtle's committee filled up the fake cave with provisions stolen at night from the floor below. Each ape exercised restraint: no ape stole from the piles made in the cave.

On the fourth night I gathered the apes together. "Tonight is the night," I said.

"It's not for nothing that my name is Solomon," Solomon began. "Wait until tomorrow night. There will be a dark moon tomorrow night. Take my word for it."

"Tonight!" I insisted. "The humans see that we have calmed down again. That is what they think anyway. They will take another ape, and then another, to join Otto and Hortense, if we do not leave."

"The signs are better for tomorrow, believe me," Solomon said.

The apes murmured. They agreed with Solomon.

"All right," I said. "Tomorrow night."

The next day took a long time to come and took a long time to pass. I urged the apes to rest and sleep for at night we would have to be alert and ready to flee.

"Tomorrow night," Solomon said after I had begun to assemble the apes after dark. "Tomorrow night will be better. The moon will be even darker."

"No! The moon will be lighter. Tonight!"

Most of the apes made fear signs. I could see that the hair on most of their backs stood erect.

"I am afraid, too," I said. "But more afraid to stay. It must be tonight or it will not be. Overcome your fears. I must overcome mine."

"Tomorrow!" Solomon insisted. Other apes repeated Solomon. They commenced to gather around him. "Tomorrow," he kept saying.

"For you, tomorrow," I said. "For me, and other fearful apes like myself who have made a decision to leave, tonight!"

Solomon lumbered over to me. He gave me the keys. "Go, if you wish," Solomon said. "Tomorrow will be better."

I started to the door. Twelve or so apes came behind me. I did not look to see who they were, but I knew their number from the sounds they made. I unlocked the door and opened it. Four of those who followed scampered back to the group around Solomon. I turned.

"Go," I said. "Those who are coming, go. I go last." Four more apes scampered back to Solomon. This left Myrtle and Moses and Lollipop and Dylys. Each went down the stairs. Moses had a hard time and almost fell; his size made this inevitable, but in addition, he had never had to move down stairs before. I turned to Solomon and all the other apes. "Tonight is the night," I said. Solomon came to me and made the friendship gesture and I made it back.

The apes who were leaving waited for me at the bottom of the stairs. I joined them and led them to the outside door. I unlocked it. "Go," I said. "Wait outside. Don't move. I will take the keys back to Solomon and return."

"Sasha," Myrtle said, "I'll take them back."

I looked hard at that ape. "You're not coming?"

Myrtle looked hard at me. "Maybe Solomon's right. To-morrow would be better."

Myrtle took the keys. She tickled me, and I tickled her back. That Myrtle was one good ape-friend. I wished she were coming. She closed the door. We could hear it lock. There the four of us were, each with a sack of supplies, though Lollipop had a hard time holding hers and Dylys took it from her right away.

"Stay close, Lollipop," Dylys said. "No jumping around here and there."

2
FREEDOM

THERE are nights without shadows. The moon is a narrow line in the sky, and even that line gets obscured by clouds that fill the sky with long arms that touch the earth and tell those brave enough to be out on such a night that there is no distance between the earth and the space around the earth. The attempts people make to brighten such nights are feeble. On the university campus there are streetlamps. The clouds came low enough to wrap themselves around those lights on the night I led Moses and Dylys and Lollipop out of the gymnasium. We stayed close to the gymnasium wall for several minutes. Moses was the first to move away. There are great trees on the campus. I could see that Moses had either seen them or smelled them and was moving toward one close to the gymnasium. I went after him.

"No," I said. I took Moses' hand, to lead him back to the side of the gymnasium. He pulled away from me, and smacked me, too. I tumbled over. "No," I repeated. I knew I wasn't giving off the fear signs. I put my hand in his again, got up and led him back to the gymnasium.

"What was it?" Dylys asked.

45

"Moses wanted to climb to the top. There are no ceilings here," I said. Lollipop was hiding behind Dylys, afraid to be near Moses. Moses sat, breathing heavily.

"Will it be all right?" Dylys asked.

"In a while," I said.

Dylys went to Moses. Lollipop ran to me, to hide. Dylys rubbed the back of Moses' head. "We forgot," she said. "You're a natural, and we forgot."

Moses' breathing got more regular as Dylys kept rubbing him. "I was in a habitat," she said. "I know what fun it is to climb. For me, it was to hide from humans. That's why they got rid of me. None of the humans ever got a look at me." She ape-smiled. I ape-laughed. Lollipop relaxed. She stayed behind me, but kept peering at Moses, looking friendly and curious. Moses, calm now, nodded. I thought he might go to sleep.

"Moses," I said. He looked at me. "We've got to stay here for many minutes. Maybe an hour. It's good and dark here, and none of us knows anything about this place. We've got to crouch here in the dark and think deep, and smell deep, and listen for humans who might come our way. We can't run for it until we get a sign about the best way to run. Do you understand?"

"Yes," Moses said. It was his first word in our old ape language.

"Good," I said. I did not want to call attention to his word.

"He talks!" Lollipop shrieked. "Just like us. He . . . "

Dylys put her hand over Lollipop's mouth. "Of course he talks. Every ape talks."

"He never did before," Lollipop said.

"Maybe you didn't understand what he said before."

46

"I never heard him say a thing before! Oh, this is great! He talks!" Lollipop started to tumble back and forth against the gymnasium. She ended up next to Moses. "Hello," she said.

Moses stared at Lollipop. He was silent.

Several minutes passed. If the truth can be known, and it can, I didn't know exactly where we should go. The sign I was looking for was not one from the heavens. It would be carried by the wind. I would smell where most of the humans were and we would go in the opposite way. The night was on our side and if our luck held, we could move away from the buildings without being seen.

"Stay here," I said. "Be very quiet."

I moved from the gymnasium. I went to another side of the building. It was as quiet there as it was in the back. Just a soft breeze, and the sound of leaves as they moved, rubbing against one another, then apart, and together again. It is a gentle sound and I sat for many minutes listening to it. I had never been alone before. Moses and Dylys and Lollipop were not far away, just around the corner, so I wasn't truly alone. Yet I could have gone away at that moment, thinking only about myself and not the others. At best, this escape was going to be hard, and more likely, it would be impossible. With four, the chances were great that we would be found out. With only one, myself, there might be a chance to go far away, where I would find some naturals and live with them.

I hated myself for having these thoughts. I had tried to get *every* ape to escape. In the first hour of freedom I thought of deserting my companions, the only ones brave enough to come with me. An ape can feel guilt. It is a burden we share with humans, particularly Catholics and Jews.

I heard the first sound other than leaves. I stopped thinking of deserting the others and rushed to them.

"Somebody is coming," I said.

"Who?" Lollipop yelled.

"Shhh, Lollipop," I said. "I don't know."

We stretched out along the gymnasium wall, close to it.

"If it's a dog, that animal will smell us, Sasha," Dylys said. "And perhaps rush at us."

"I don't like dogs," Lollipop said.

"You've never seen one," Dylys said.

"I have a feeling I don't like them. Let's go back inside," Lollipop said.

I reached out to Lollipop and drew her close to me.

"Thanks," she said. "I'll shut up."

"Good ape," I said. "Quiet now."

The sound got closer.

"It's not a dog," I whispered. "I think it's a human. I can hear sounds like human sounds. I'll look around the corner."

"No," Dylys said. "Hold Lollipop. I'll look." She scampered noiselessly to the corner of the gymnasium, turned and was out of sight. In a few seconds she came back. "It's a human. He is coming this way."

"Is he one of those we have seen inside?" I asked.

"It's hard to know."

There was nothing to do but huddle against the gymnasium and hope the human would not come close to us. Even in the dark, and without shadows, Moses loomed huge. If the human came anywhere near, he would see

48

Moses and Moses would have to protect us. I sensed that Moses knew of this possibility. He gave no fear signs, so I hoped, for his own sake, the human would not come upon us. Especially if he was one not connected with the experiment. Yes, apes are generally well-disposed toward humans, in spite of what humans have done to and with us. It is not in our nature to curse humans because of the follies of a few of their number. That is a characteristic of humans, and one of their least attractive ones.

From the walking sounds the human made, I guessed he had a 78% drowsy degree. He was dragging along, and not walking as a young human would walk. And he kept stopping. He made sounds, but they were not words. He made singing sounds. Dylys went to the corner of the gymnasium again.

"He's stopping here and there," she whispered back. "He carries a bottle and drinks from it."

I went to the corner, too. Lollipop was clinging to me.

"Look," Dylys said, "he's sitting down against that tree. Why is he doing that?"

I knew right away that this was a human made strange by alcohol. Many apes have been associated with experiments involving alcohol—whiskey, gin, vodka and the like. The experiments are designed to help humans understand what happens to their bodies when they drink much alcohol. It is a terrible experiment for an ape to be associated with, and all apes are fearful that one day they will be taken for an alcohol experiment. It is the final experiment, we say. Perhaps, when and if the other apes learn about the experiment we are associated with, another experiment will be labeled the final experiment. Perhaps not. It is more a human, rather than ape, characteristic to conclude that something is final. When we use the word *final*, we use it in the sense of "most terrible," rather than "last." We know that humans have dreams of perfection. Our dreams are more modest.

"He is drunk," I said. "He is no danger to us."

Lollipop dropped off me. She peered through the dark at the man sitting against the tree. "Why does he sit there like that?" she asked.

"He's taking a rest, Lollipop," Dylys said.

"And another drink," I said as the man lifted his bottle to his mouth.

The man drank. Then he began to make soft noises again. "Da da, da da da, da da da," he seemed to be saying. He reached into a pocket and brought out a small bag. He dipped his hand into it, and ate whatever it was that was in it.

"I'm hungry!" Lollipop screamed. She sprang away from us, running to the man.

"Lollipop!" Dylys called. Dylys began to run after Lollipop. I grabbed her and held her back. "What if . . . ?" Dylys said.

"No!" I said. Lollipop got to the man. We could see that he shook his head. I felt the fear signs coming from Dylys. I felt her trying to pull loose. Moses came up behind us. "Wait!" I insisted.

Lollipop put out her hand.

"Je . . . sus!" the man said.

Lollipop grabbed the paper bag the man held.

"Je . . . sus," he said again.

Lollipop was gobbling up whatever was in the bag. She tore apart the bag and licked the inside. She ripped it into pieces and tossed the pieces about.

"I'm afraid," Dylys said.

Lollipop tried to grab the bottle the man held. He did not let go of it. He held himself rigid against the tree. Lollipop kept pulling at the bottle.

"Lollipop," Dylys called out. Dylys broke away from me. She ran to Lollipop and snatched her up in her arms.

"Je . . . sus!" the man said once again.

I went after Dylys and Lollipop. Moses was behind me. The man gave off terrible fear signs. He kept trying to push, push, push himself into the tree. Dylys backed off, holding Lollipop close to her. The man jumped up suddenly and ran into the night. I was wrong about his drowsy degree. He had a 20% drowsy degree.

There was no longer any possibility of lingering close to the gymnasium. The man filled with alcohol might report what he had seen. Even if nobody believed him, it was too dangerous to take the chance. I would have to guess which would be the best route to get us away from people. I was not ready. There were not enough smells to give me an idea or clues. Low clouds and damp air inhibit smells.

"There are more streetlights to the right," I said. "That probably means there are more people that way."

"If we go to the left, we'll be following that man," Dylys said. "But it's darker that way."

We got our sacks of supplies. I led the way. Dylys took Lollipop's hand. Moses came last. We moved quickly from tree to tree. I would go to one, stop for a second or so to see what might lie ahead, and run to the next. Dylys and Lollipop followed my exact same route. And so did Moses. We went for several hundred yards in this way. I motioned the other three to join me.

"There hasn't been anyone," Dylys said.

"This is fun," Lollipop said. She was out of breath.

"We'll go that way," I said, pointing to the left. "The trees there in the distance are closer together than here. I don't see any buildings, either."

"I'll go first," Dylys said. "You look after Lollipop."

"I don't need looking after," Lollipop said. "It's him," she said, pointing at Moses, "that needs looking after. He moves like an elephant, not an ape. I'm the fastest one here, I'll betcha."

Moses punched Lollipop. Softly, very softly, to be sure, but enough to knock her over. We all ape-laughed, except for Lollipop. "You big ape!" Lollipop shouted. We ape-laughed even more. Dylys picked up Lollipop and gave her a friendly hug. She passed her to me and I gave her a friendly hug. I made a motion to pass her to Moses. "No!" Lollipop said. "Not him."

We were off again, Dylys leading the way. She was a better lead ape than I was anyway. She was lighter and moved with a softer footfall than I. Moses had the worst time. He was so heavy that twigs and leaves cracked and made noise under his weight. He also carried most of the supplies. Even in the dark, he made a big silhouette, his great bulk plodding noisily on, over earth Dylys scarcely touched, she was so agile. When he would come close, I would stare at him, and into his great black eyes that had seen the faraway lands. I was thinking of the stories he would tell us when we got away and were safe.

We moved into a place where the trees got closer and closer together. There were many low bushes, as well. Here it was easier to move unseen, but the bushes were noisy and made it hard for us to see far ahead. I think we must have moved into a woods, not a forest far from everything, but a stretch of dense growth. We were still close to the university. In the distance there was a sound that I associate with humans—an automobile racing along the streets. This sound is especially terrifying to apes. Many apes have seen automobiles. They have heard stories of the great dangers automobiles make. They know of their speed and weight. Any ape who has heard of automobiles wants to stay far from them. Apes would never make an object that would destroy other apes in the way humans have made automobiles that destroy other humans. This is one of the thousands of ways in which apes and humans are unalike. In the faraway lands, we are told, there is much destruction and violence. There, we are told, there is a purpose to terrible events. It is to preserve an ape's territory, and to make more apes, and to protect the infant apes. Humans, we have heard, destroy each other by accident on roads. What can be more terrifying than to destroy another accidentally?

"This is a good place," Dylys said.

"In what way?" I asked.

"The trees are close and we can hide in the bushes," she said.

I saw Lollipop begin to rip at some of the bushes. She put a few leaves in her mouth but spat them out. "Ugh," she said. She was having a good time ripping up some other leaves.

"We don't stay here," I said.

"There are more dark hours," Moses said.

Dylys and Lollipop and I looked deep at Moses. None of us said anything. So, that big ape now knew many of the ancient ape-words. Was it fitting to say something to

him? Can you congratulate an ape because he has re-
verted? If Moses had been a less formidable ape, it would
have been appropriate to say something about the words
he had mastered. Or even to suggest that he let us captives
know how it was that naturals spoke to each other in the
faraway places. Many captives would have welcomed
the chance to know ape language as it is now spoken. It
could serve us in ways that the human language that we
master so readily could never serve *us*, whatever this
mastery may mean to humans. These were solemn
thoughts for me.

"Moses is right," I said. "We should move as far from
the university as we can, while we can. Even if the man
filled with alcohol does not tell humans about us, in the
morning the graduate students will know we are gone."

We moved on, Dylys leading as before. We made more
noise than we had, because of the bushes. If there had
been a bright and full moon, it would have been easier.
But it was because there was not that we had got this far,
I was sure.

We walked for an hour. We stopped for several minutes,
resting one against the other. Lollipop fell asleep.

"It will be morning soon," Moses said.

We continued. I carried Lollipop on my back. She
made sleep noises. Occasionally she would struggle to be
let loose and would fall to the earth. I picked her up each
time. As we went on, we knew that we had left the university far behind. We were climbing. There were no
automobile sounds, and very few other sounds. We had
gone a great distance when it got light.

"Now is the time to hide," Dylys said. "We take turns
sleeping. Except for Lollipop." We ape-laughed. We found

a place, high on a hill, looking over miles of countryside. Moses began to gather leaves. He climbed into a tree to make a sleeping nest there. We looked at him with interest, and did the same. Neither Dylys nor Lollipop nor I had ever had to make our sleeping places before. Lollipop asked if she might share Dylys' nest with her. We saw the university far away, and the many buildings that surrounded it. We saw how close we had come to other buildings in our long walk from the gymnasium. Some were small and must have had humans in them. I wondered what ape protector had led us this far, what all-seeing spirit from the faraway places had known of our trek and had darkened the night and made every restless creature in it silent, so that we could get this far away from the experiment. Apes believe that certain things are inevitable, while other things are not meant to be. That morning— what there was of morning then—I was certain that what had happened already, and would happen in the days ahead, was inevitable.

I took the first watch, filling my mind with thoughts of the past and the future. When the sun came in view, it carried with it a message from my ancestors and the faraway lands. That is the way with the sun, and with the moon, stars, rain and wind if we look at and feel them deeply.

Dylys and Moses took their turns on watch. By the time the sun was at its high point, Lollipop was ready to scamper about and play. Both Dylys and I were asleep. Lollipop had a lot of fun waking us up. Lollipop, like Myrtle, favored the tickle game above all others. She wasn't ready to tickle Moses but did not mind waking Dylys or me. She bounced from one to the other of us, first tickling our feet, then our bellies, then our arms. Dylys was the first to grab Lollipop. She tickled that little ape fiercely. Lollipop could hardly stand it, she was so deliriously happy. She even sprang for an instant toward Moses, still on watch, but as soon as he looked at her she backed off.

Next Lollipop grabbed one of the sacks of supplies. She tipped it so that everything fell out. She started taking one bite from one thing and another bite from something else.

"No, Lollipop," Dylys said, "it's not like back there. The food has got to last a long time. Take just a little and give some to Sasha and Moses and me."

"I'm very hungry," Lollipop said.

"We're all hungry," Dylys said. "Moses must get the most to eat. Look at what a big space he has to fill."

"That's not fair," Lollipop said. "I'm still a baby. I get the most."

"And Moses carried most of the stuff, too," I said. "Remember that, Lollipop."

Lollipop sat silently for two minutes. She had taken bites from five pieces of food and they were scattered around her. She took one of them to Dylys and put it in her hand. Dylys patted Lollipop on the head. Lollipop took two pieces to Moses, who took them as his due. She brought two to me. I drew her close. I was squatting on the ground and she fit snugly between my legs. Her back was resting against my belly. I began to eat: one bite for me, one bite down to Lollipop, who twisted her head so she could look up at me eating. When we finished, I played the tickle game with Lollipop for several minutes.

"Quiet!" Moses said. We stopped the game. Dylys and

Lollipop and I stared at Moses. He was making mighty sniffs. "Something is coming," Moses said. Lollipop ran to Dylys. I got off the ground and went to Moses. "Listen," he said. Moses was right. There were sounds nearby. Not regular sounds that would accompany a steady footfall, but sounds that would last for some seconds and stop, only to begin again and stop. With each new sound, whoever or whatever it was got closer to us. I looked around to get a better feel of where we were and where we should be. Our sleeping place had been good because it was far up in the hills and beyond where humans would come. But that was at dawn, and now it was many hours later. Maybe we had left a trail as we made our way from the university through the woods below and up into the hills. Maybe the man filled with alcohol had not really run away from us, but only run out of our sight. Maybe he was able to tell the scientists where we had gone and now they would come and take us back to the gymnasium. It would be easy for them. All they need do is see us from a distance and fire their dope guns at us, as they had with Moses to give him examinations. They could put us to sleep in seconds and a great number of them could come into the hills and carry us away. They would have a hard time with Moses, but not with me or Dylys or Lollipop. I looked around at the trees. They were not as high as below, but there were some with great growth that would cover us if we climbed high enough and stayed silent. They had proved to be excellent sleeping places. I pointed to a high tree that sprang from the ground in a dip in the hill. Of all the trees nearby, it was the biggest and most full.

"Up," I whispered to Dylys. Dylys, Lollipop clinging to her, grabbed a low branch and pulled herself into the tree. She made her way upward until she was hidden by the growth in the low part of the tree.

I grabbed one of our sacks, and Moses took two others. There was not time to put together the supplies Lollipop had scattered about from the fourth sack. I climbed into the tree with Dylys and Lollipop. When Moses grabbed the lowest branch, we could hear it crack. As he swung his great bulk on the branch, it cracked even more. The sounds we heard coming toward us stopped for more than their usual few seconds each time the branch cracked, but resumed after a pause. Moses went to look for a stronger tree. I could not help for I was surrounded with leaves and could not see farther than the trees closest to us. The sound of the stranger came closer. We would see its source in seconds. Moses fled over soft grass. He could not be heard.

I looked down. The stranger stood directly under the tree where we three apes were perched. I did not know what kind of creature this was. At least it was not a human. It had size. It was bigger than I, but not as big as Moses. This thought gave me some relief. The creature stood on four legs. It moved in swift, jerky motions; its head—at the end of a long neck, like on a horse I had once seen, and with great protruding ears—kept moving forward and back. It paused every few seconds to look around, and then kept pulling at leaves on the low bushes. It saw the supplies. Waiting several seconds, it sniffed the air, then the ground around the supplies, and finally some of the food lying there. Lollipop squirmed in Dylys' arms. Leaves nearby stirred and the creature looked up from the supplies. It turned to look behind and moved ahead some steps. Lollipop stirred again, and so did the leaves on Dylys' branch. Now, for the first time, the creature looked up. Our eyes met. I saw fear in the eyes of the creature. It stood rooted to the ground, staring at me. Perhaps no time passed. To me, it seemed like an eternity. There are moments, we apes believe, when a being's whole existence is open for the world to see. Such moments come in one's last hours, we believe, but for some rare few, at other times in their lives, too. This was such a moment in my life, and in the life of the creature below. That creature saw all of my ancestors, knew every place I had been and knew what would happen in my future. And I knew the same of it, without knowing, even, what kind of creature this was. This moment passed as the creature turned abruptly and bolted away with such speed that it was hard to know if we had seen it at all.

"It was a deer," Dylys said when we had come down from the tree and Moses had returned. "A female deer. I used to see them in the habitat. There was nothing to fear."

We made a plan. The others would stay where we had stopped while I went on to a higher place to see farther away. When I found the best way for us to go, I would come back to get the others. As no humans had yet come, there was a chance that none would come; if any did, Dylys and Lollipop could climb into the big tree and Moses could disappear for a time, as he had done when the deer came to our resting place. I would be back before dark, and could lead us in the best direction.

"What if you do not return?" Dylys asked.

"I will."

"But if not?" she said.

"Moses will take care of you and Lollipop," I said. Moses nodded.

I made the friendship gesture to Dylys and she made it back; I made it to Moses and he made it back; and to Lollipop, who made it back three times. It was the first time another ape had made the friendship gesture to her, she said.

I set my eyes on the higher hills in the distance. I would go to one and take a look at the world around here. Lollipop came with me a very little way, still within sight of Dylys and Moses. "Go back now, Lollipop," I said. She pulled my hand a few times and we both ape-laughed.

I turned to see that Lollipop got back safely. For an instant I wanted to go back to the others and tell them the plan was no good, that we should stay together at all times. But I knew the plan was a sensible one and would save our time and our energy. Moses was too unaccustomed to humans' ways to go scouting; besides, he would protect Dylys and Lollipop in formidable ways that were not available to me. And so, I left them.

At first my concern was how long it would take me to get to one of the highest hills and to get back before dark. Without the others to think about, I could move more quickly than before. Besides, the sun was still high and there was no need to puzzle every minute about the next few paces. Everything was clear just in front of me, and far beyond, perhaps for miles. All I needed to do was note my path so that I might return easily. Still, in these hills nearly everything looked alike. There were stretches of open land; dips in the land; places where there were many trees; and other places where only a thick growth grew, clinging low to the ground and making the passage difficult. At first I remembered the spaces I passed through. As I passed more and more of them, it was not clear to me if I had been there already, or was passing through a new place that looked like many others. I fixed my eyes on a high hill in the distance and vowed to myself that I would look at it, and it alone, until I got to it and climbed it. This proved to be a foolish resolve for I kept tripping on the low growth and bumping into trees and great rocks.

Two hours passed in this way and still the great hill was far from me. I could see that the sun had reached the top of it and that the hill changed the sun's color; such was the power of this great hill before me. I must reach it.

The sun disappeared behind the hill. I knew I could not chase it, for soon the hill would cast a long shadow over the land in front of it and afterward dark would come. I had come a long way from the other apes, and had discovered nothing.

And I was alone. Not alone, as I had been last night, for a few moments only, but alone and apart. I stopped to think about being alone. As before, I told myself that I could make out better alone than with the others. Why this idea came back to me again I don't know. But it did. Who was Moses? A huge natural whose size called attention to him in countless ways. True, he had learned the old language and had done everything that he had had to do since last night. But Moses was an outstanding creature! How long could we go on unobserved as long as Moses was with us? As for Dylys, good ape that she was, wouldn't it be better not to have the responsibility of her? Lollipop's antics would lead us to disaster. These thoughts, and others, raced through my head as I knew that I could not

61

reach the great hill and be back to the others before dark. That was almost here.

So I sat in some low growth. I pulled at the leaves around me and ate a few of them. They had a sweet taste, satisfying in many ways. I knew that I could live on such leaves and other good things that I might find.

I knew, too, that *we* could live from the land.

The dark came and I stayed where I had stopped. Dylys and Moses and Lollipop would be expecting me now. I could feel that they were listening for me. I looked to the sky and saw that the slim line of a moon that had been our friend the night before was still as slim as it had been then. I got up and began to head back to the sleeping place. It was dark and hard going. There were numerous small hills in front of me. Which was the one that I had come from? I kept looking for signs that I had come this way or that, an hour or two before, but no signs came to me. I was lost. It was my wish come true. Now there was a reason to go on by myself. I did not know where my companions were or how I could reach them.

A sign came. The world got lit up by the flash that comes before a rain storm. The flash pointed to a particular hill, and I took it as a message from my ancestors that that was the hill I had left earlier. There could be no other reason for the flash and the great noise that followed it. I fixed my eye on that hill, waiting for the rain that would come, and made my way to it.

The rain never came. It was a time when signs in the sky, and the noise that follows those signs, deceive those on earth. Now I know the reason for those strange signs. It is because there are creatures wandering in the dark, in need of a light to direct them. These signs, frequent as they are, suggest that many wander the earth in darkness, seeking signs.

The flash came again. And again. Each flash brought me closer to the hill I had left. And finally to our resting place of the night before.

"Dylys," I said softly.

There was no answer.

"Dylys," I said again.

It was quiet still.

"Moses? Lollipop?" I said.

Still no answer. I went to the big tree, where Dylys and Lollipop would be likely to hide if they heard a strange noise. "Dylys?" I said, looking up. "Lollipop?"

I climbed the tree. No ape was there. "Dylys!" I called out. "Lollipop! Moses!"

Oh, the many, many things I do not know. I came down from the tree where I had looked for Dylys and Lollipop and sat on the ground underneath it. I ran my arm up and down the bottom part of that tree over and over again. It is a belief among apes that if we touch places associated with lost ones we will learn their whereabouts. This is one of many beliefs that naturals have brought with them from the faraway lands. Captives, in their situations, seldom have chances to test any of these beliefs. We accept them as our own, for naturals have no reason to lie. In this way we build a sense of our past, even though we have none that any of us captives can remember. Years, generations, perhaps even centuries may have passed between the first ape in a line of apes who left the faraway lands, and its descendants who are alive today. Can you

63

wonder why descendants grasp at superstitions and try to make them parts of their lives, as though these beliefs were their own discovered knowledge?

No sign came to me. I left the tree and wandered around the sleeping place. There were leavings from the supplies we had eaten before, but the sacks were gone. Would that mean that Moses and Dylys and Lollipop had time to gather together the supplies and left in an orderly way? Or did it mean that they had been discovered by humans, who gathered the supplies and took them with the apes back to the gymnasium?

Should I wait, and hope that they would come back? Should I guess in which direction they went, and try to find them? Should I go back to the gymnasium, either to find out what happened or to give myself up? As for this last possibility, as soon as it crossed my mind I dismissed it.

When decisions have always been made for us, it is difficult and terrifying suddenly to make decisions ourselves. Humans are trained to make decisions, to think deep and to determine, from among possibilities, that one course is better than another. Captive apes have no such training. That is why, back at the gymnasium, old Solomon could not bring himself to escape with us. He had spent his life pretending to have wisdom and knowledge, but because he never had big decisions to make, when the moment came he was filled with awful fear and terror. This observation is no criticism of Solomon, or of his intelligence and bravery. If your life has no challenge, when the moment comes, it appears safest to back away from all challenge. There has been no training for it. What an ancestor there must have been in the faraway land that I might have come from; what a creature he or she must have been to plant this seed within me; what a restless nature I have.

Dylys, too.

And even little Lollipop.

And Moses.

"Where are you, apes?" I called out.

I climbed the tree where Dylys and Lollipop and I had hidden ourselves from the deer. I sat in it for many hours. The night had sounds that I had not heard the night before, when our minds were not on the solitary noises that may have filled the air. Now each seemed more mysterious than the one before it. Sometimes there would be a quick movement in the grass; sometimes a night bird would howl; often there was a swooping movement through the air; and there were cries of creatures that had been silent before. It was dark that night, as it had been dark the night before. My mind was filled with dark thoughts.

When dawn came I climbed down from the tree where I had passed the night with my thoughts. What a heavy heart I had. As no ape had come back to this place, I would go on alone. I looked around for a long time. Our first night alone together had been spent here. It seemed a part of history. I went to where I had stood the watch, and after me Dylys, and after her Moses. I remembered how it was that Lollipop got more to eat than all of us; I remembered her face as she sat against my belly, looking up at me as I ate. I remembered the eyes of that female deer who knew what would happen to me today and in the future. As I moved away from our sleeping place, the gray light of the earliest part of morning changed. Many thousands of birds had made their morning noises, calling for the sun, and it finally appeared in the sky far beyond the university and the lands that stretched before it. I wondered where I would be when it moved behind the greatest hills today.

My first moments on the trail were filled with feelings of guilt. It is as I said before: apes share this ability, or disability, with humans. I was sure that I had failed my companions. In wishing twice that I might be alone, mysterious forces had heard me and fulfilled my wish. It was a bad wish; more a speculation than a wish, I told myself. Every ape has asked, "What if . . . ?" It is in the nature of captive apes to concern themselves with alternatives to the terrible fates humans design for them. Apes spend hours among themselves asking futile "What if . . . ?" questions. From such games, apes gain a certain dignity: they are able to share with other apes their conception of themselves. Most often apes wish to be in the faraway lands of their ancestors. They imagine their lives there with their ancient families and among places made familiar and comfortable to them by the centuries.

After a while I began to think I might notice a sign here or there that my companions had passed this way. I saw nothing and ran back to my starting point. I looked carefully at the grass and low growth. Moses was a huge ape and would have been certain to make signs, however inadvertently, here and there. Sure enough, I could see that they had set out after me, following the line I took yesterday. I hurried to the place I parted from Lollipop and saw more signs of their passing. They must have determined that they would follow me in a straight line. If

I had come back to the sleeping place by the same route I left, we would have met. I must have come back on a different path. It was only because there were flashes of light that I got back at all. Perhaps that is why they were not there when I returned. Perhaps, in the faraway lands, Moses had never before seen flashes of light and heard the loud noise that follows. Dylys may have been fearful, along with Moses and Lollipop. My spirits brightened. I would see places that Moses had passed: the undergrowth would be trampled, branches would be freshly broken and there would be indications in various other ways that a great creature had passed this way. If I moved fast and did not pause for rests, I would be sure to catch up with them. Various things, and particularly Lollipop, would point to a slow passage in which caution would be important. If they walked through the night they would leave even more obvious signs than during the day. Perhaps, with the dawn, they had rested. Perhaps I would reach them before the sun got to the top of the world.

It proved easy to follow their path. Even in the open areas the grass was broken. I ape-laughed in anticipation of seeing my companions. Never again would I have the wish to be alone.

My pace got faster. I thought of calling out but reasoned that it was too soon. I had spent the night, many hours between my return to the sleeping place and leaving, and my friends would have moved on throughout all the time I pondered my fate in the tree in that place. Somewhere ahead, Lollipop was sleeping, while either Dylys or Moses kept watch. I would call out. Later.

My spirits continued to rise. When, rarely, I seemed to lose the path, it was easy to pick it up again. I tired. I squatted for a moment or two. It was tempting to curl myself up in some bushes or to make a nest in a tree and dream good ape-dreams. Each time the temptation got most intense, I remembered my friends and ran on.

An hour passed in this way. And then another. And another. I must be near them.

"Moses!" I called. "Dylys!"

There was no answer. The morning sounds had quieted by now. The birds squawked only rarely, and quieter noises were everywhere, insect noises that flourish in the heat of the day.

"I'm here," I called out. "It's Sasha!"

The creature came at me from nowhere. I thought it was a wolf. Perhaps a fox. I did not know. It sprang at me. Was it a lion? A lynx? How could I tell? What did it matter? It had thick legs and mighty claws that ripped against my chest and tore me. I shrieked, in surprise at first, and, in a moment, in pain. The creature sprang at me again. I moved aside and it fell to the ground. I put my long arms in front of me to keep it away from me. The creature tried to hit my arms aside. I began to slash at it. It could not get close to me, my arms were swinging so rapidly and with such violence. I made terrible noises and so did the creature. I saw that the earth in front of me was beginning to be covered with my blood. The sight made me make noises more terrible than before. My arms had a great violence in them. "Moses!" I yelled for myself, "I have the strength of Moses!" All of that ape's power came into my arms. I had never fought another creature before. This was a death-fight. My death or the death of this creature. I must hold it off with one arm and do it in with the other. All I had were my arms. I grabbed the creature by its throat, and it slashed my arm. Blood was everywhere, from me, from it. "Moses!" I called again. "I have his strength!" I drew my free arm back to come down on the creature's neck. When I got it firmly in my grasp I did not make the final blow. I picked up the creature by its neck and throat and threw it aside. I waited for it to rush at me again, but nothing happened. I could hear the creature in the undergrowth. It was moving away. Each of us trailed blood behind us, for I moved away as quickly as I could.

I knew, now, what it would be like here in the hills. "Dylys," I called weakly. "Moses." I heard myself repeating their names over and over as I went on, following their trail. But I lost the trail. I fell to the ground, thinking nothing.

What a strange and unusual sensation it was, this warmth moving over my chest, and onto my arms, and back again to my chest. Over and over again. Why wasn't the creature ripping at me? Why this gentle warmth? What? Why?

I raised myself slowly. I opened my eyes but had no thought as I did. I did not think about what I would see or if I would see anything.

"He is awake," I heard Dylys say. And then, louder, "Moses, Sasha is awake."

Now I saw her. And squatting next to her, Lollipop. Then Moses came behind them. He cast a great shadow over us all. He sat. He reached over to touch me. He ran his arm here and there over my body. He nodded at me, and I at him.

"I licked," Lollipop said.

"I know, Lollipop," I said. "I could feel you."

"Did you?"

"Yes," I said. I rubbed her head. She came close. She licked my chest. "That is why I am here, Lollipop, because of you and Dylys and Moses. Thank you."

I tried to get up. It was too soon. I fell back onto the ground. We all ape-laughed.

And so they told me the story. It was as I had imagined. When the dark came that night, and I had not returned, they set out to meet me on the path. They did not know there was no prescribed path until it was too late. They went for many miles. They debated—Moses and Dylys—about going back to the sleeping place. But it was night and there was no way for them to retrace their route.

"And we talked, too," Dylys said, "about some terrible things that could have happened."

Dylys was on the watch when she heard the noises of the fight between me and that creature. She said those noises filled the air. All the wild ones in the hills, the birds, too, made shrieking sounds. All were filled with the terror of that moment.

"Here," Dylys said, "it happens quickly. There is a sound for a second or two, and then nothing. Out here they are accustomed to quickness."

"How long was it?" I asked.

"Many minutes," Dylys said. "Moses went for you. The sun has been in the sky two times since he brought you to this sleeping place."

"Two times," I said to myself.

"Did you really know it was me licking?" Lollipop asked.

"Yes."

"She licked, too," Lollipop said, looking at Dylys. "So did Moses."

"I know," I said.

So, this is what it was like, being free of humans. The thought had been the last one on my mind after my combat. I did not know what to do with that thought now. Should I hate humans for making it impossible for us when we are apart from their lives? Should I value them for protecting us, and for feeding us, whatever the reasons? What is the difference between being torn apart by a strange creature in these hills and what happens in the gymnasium many miles away? I am not a philosophical ape, but a practical one. I do not want abstract answers to questions. I want sensible answers to those questions. Is my life of less value than a human's because humans dominate everywhere? Does the world exist for humans? Or is there an order to the world that humans have ruined? Who has the answers?

"Moses has the biggest tongue in the world," Lollipop said.

"I know," I said, "and it is wonderful. But so is Dylys'. And so, especially, is yours."

"Thank you," Lollipop said.

In two days I began to feel like my former self. We had had to stay in this new sleeping place for a long time and it was filled with our signs. We learned that most animals in the hills busy themselves finding food, digging holes, taking care of each other. Sometimes when an animal

71

came our way we would see it stop, terrified by the sight of us, and run away. We had many good ape-laughs when that happened. More frequently, an animal would pause for some moments to determine if we meant harm. Concluding that we did not, it continued its pursuits. We wondered who these interesting, independent creatures were, and if they had names and what their habits were. None spoke ape language.

Lollipop found a tiny creature that would walk up her arm and back down to the earth again. It would run on its four legs, stand for a second and then resume its travels. The creature gave Lollipop extreme pleasure, and it came back two times after a first visit. Lollipop did not want to let it go away so she tried to sit on it. It scampered off, not pausing to stand, and did not return.

"We'll go now," Moses said at last. "We'll stay together."

We walked for many hours, resting here and there. We came to the bottom of the greatest hill and slept, with a watch out as always. On the next day we climbed the hill. When we ended our climb we were at the top of the world. We looked everywhere. There were other great hills in the distance, and low lands among them. Here and there we could see a building made by a human. We turned away from those buildings.

"That is the way," Moses said, pointing to a hill lower than this one and covered with trees and bushes. A thin line of water rushed among the trees, over great rocks, sometimes falling a distance to land in a pool.

———

3
HOME

IT is not in the nature of an ape to stay in one small place. We have been taught by humans how accommodations may be made. They take care of us. They house and feed us for the various purposes humans have. They believe that they can study us, make us entertain, exhibit us, etc., etc., to good advantage when we are in fixed places. They have a notion that they have "captured" us. Reflective apes—I am not one of them, as I have mentioned before—say that whatever it is the humans want from us will be something they will never get. In violating our nature, which is to roam from place to place, enjoying the land and the trees and the great bounty the earth offers to us all, humans lose the exact thing they expect to learn or gain from us. When an ape is caged, humans may believe that their understanding of our and their natures is richer from studying apes like myself, born in San Diego. Humans err. They increase their understanding of creatures of their own creation. They do not increase their understanding of apes, or of humans, the true object of these various experiments and programs. Reflective apes tell me that humans are doomed to fail, whatever their intentions, in almost everything they pursue. I have never been able to accept such a cynical view of humans. Humans are earnest. However ill-mannered most seem, there are those among them who want to make the world, and, of late, the outer world, a different, richer place.

Let me give an example of how ill-comprehending humans are of nature. It is the natural condition of apes that as we foul an area where we have paused for a day or more, we move from it to a new place. We do not make "homes," even though we may mark off a big territory and claim it as our own. Other creatures, like the creature who attacked me some days ago, make homes in certain specific places. By their natures, they would not foul such homes but go far away from them in satisfying the natural demands of their bodies. In this way, some creatures come to protect small places that apes, for example, would leave in a moment. Humans do not appreciate these differences.

Apes have heard that humans talk of non-human animals as though we are of a kind. We are not. Each animal is different from each other animal, and among like animals, each animal is unlike any other. Humans are more alike than the other animals. It is necessary only for apes to overhear humans talk to know that this is true.

These observations are not just my own, but those of the more reflective apes, as well. They filled my mind as we went to the place Moses had told us we must move toward.

"Why the big rush?" Lollipop said. "I want to have some fun." Moses gave Lollipop a look. He did not slow his pace as he led us toward the site he had chosen. "Come on!" Lollipop insisted. "Let's play!" Lollipop jumped up into a tree and swung from one of the low branches. "Look," she called out, "one hand!" Moses kept his pace. He now carried three sacks of supplies; Dylys and he thought I was too weak to carry a sack. I followed Moses, and Dylys, supposedly with Lollipop in hand, followed me, in case I should stumble and need help. By rights, Dylys and Lollipop should have been in the middle. That would have been the proper way.

"We'll see you later," Dylys called out to Lollipop, still hanging in her tree, and now some distance behind us.

"No!" Lollipop shrieked. "Watch me!"

We kept on walking, and could hear Lollipop fall to the ground and scamper to catch up with us. "What a crowd," Lollipop said, jumping onto Dylys' back. "I wouldn't have come if I didn't think it was going to be fun."

"You wouldn't?" Dylys said.

"No."

"Isn't riding on my back fun?"

Lollipop was silent for a moment. "Yes," she said, "riding on your back is fun." She put her arms around Dylys' neck and lowered herself to stretch as far along Dylys' back as she could. I took the sack Dylys was carrying. It was the lightest of the four and I could carry it easily.

When Moses tired, we rested. Lollipop jumped from one to the other of us, even Moses. "This is fun," she said. "I didn't mean it when I said I wouldn't have come. I was just kidding." She tickled Moses, and ran away from him before he could do anything to her. However, I could see that he wouldn't have done anything anyway. It was not that he was tired, or lacked the will to react to Lollipop;

I could feel it about him that he did not mind Lollipop's frolics. An ape can look deep behind another ape's eyes and into his mind when that feeling of finding your brother or your sister begins to fill your own mind, and your heart as well. At that moment, resting on our path, Moses' face did not show it, nor did his eyes; but in his mind I had become his brother and he had become mine. I was startled. I kept staring at Moses, looking for a sign that he knew we were brothers, but none came. None was needed.

I turned to Dylys, and found that it did not matter what her face told me, or her eyes, either. I saw into her mind and she was my sister.

The three of us—Moses, Dylys and Sasha—sat for many moments deep in our contemplations. Lollipop continued to scamper about, and made numerous squeaks and noises, jabbering away in short ape-sentences about this and that. We all touched and comforted her. She was unaware that we were different now from a half hour ago, for we said nothing, and seemed simply to be sitting idly, resting, for that was the plan Lollipop had heard us agree to.

"Let's get going," Lollipop said. "I want to get to the place pretty soon. There's a lot of things on my mind about this place, so I want to see it for myself."

"In a little while," I could hear Dylys say softly.

We continued to sit, looking deep inside of each other. When it was time to move, we would get up and continue our trek, but this was not the time. Lollipop sat down suddenly, snuggling her belly onto Dylys' belly and falling asleep.

This new feeling pushed itself out of our minds and into our eyes. A long time passed as we took great satisfaction in looking at each other. Now, in recollection, I know that

our spirits mingled then. Whatever ape things happened thereafter to one, would happen to all.

In time we were ready to continue our way.

When humans come to a place, that place is changed in ways that make that place *for* humans. When apes and other creatures come upon a place, they accept that place for what it is already. True, an ape changes a place, but only in necessary ways. Humans change things idly. For humans, the world and the earth that covers the world exist *for* humans. They dig into it, they build great structures, they move it aside and replace it in capricious ways. Humans, we know, construe what they do to be progress. Progress is an explanation for everything. Humans are deeply confused. Change is not progress. The most simpleminded ape knows this true fact, and yet humans, for their great sophistication and knowledge, rarely examine the dark side of their so-called progress. What does it mean when humans take a great ape like Moses from the faraway lands and bring that ape to America to pull him apart to see if they can put him together again, perhaps with some other ape's parts: Myrtle's, for instance, or old Solomon's, or even mine? Can such an experiment be called progress? Yes, I know humans will say. They are taught at the youngest age to see progress in change. It is why they get their educations, and subsequently set their minds to improving the world. I dearly love their innocence, it is so sweet and short-sighted. And their great intelligence, it makes them the most stupid of all animals. This is another sad truth that all apes know.

The natural world is easy to understand and hard to

describe. It begins deep beneath the surface of the earth, and, there, is the most preserved part of the world. Humans violate these depths for the riches that are there, but for the most part it is not known by humans. They dig deeply into it, and drill into it as well, and take the things they need from it, but they have not discovered it and made it their own. Apes from the faraway lands tell many stories of ape journeys in earlier times into the center of the earth. There was a single opening in one of the faraway lands that leads to the path that in ancient days apes took on their journeys to the center of the earth. Only privileged and unusual apes were chosen for these great journeys. When the apes returned, they told all the other apes of the wonders inside, of the darks, and the great spaces, and the waters, and the places where it was so beautiful that no ape who had seen them would ever forget them. It became, in those ancient days, the greatest wish of an ape to be selected to make the journey inside. Few were chosen, as that was the natural order of things. Glorious adventures lose their glory for apes when they are common events. It happened, once, that a crafty and evil ape entered the only opening to the crucial path, and so the opening was sealed off forever, and no ape has entered the center of the earth since ancient times. All apes understand that it was just, that the opening be sealed, and grieve even today that one of our own kind would have been evil. I have said it before: perfection eludes us.

Toward the surface of the earth there are soft lands of great variety. Rich brown earths are favored by humans, for foods grow from them in both natural and artificial ways. There are sands and clays and numerous other varieties of lands, too. And water rests on the earth in profusion. Many creatures live in the waters, just as many

other creatures live in the soft lands, under the surface. In addition to the foods that spring from these rich lands, trees grow, and bushes and vines. It is a glorious thing to be in a place where humans do not disturb these things, where they are born naturally and grow—and, yes, die—undisturbed by anything other than the order of their lives, and by non-human animals who by instinct know their functions and understand relationships in nature.

Here, where Moses led us, was a place humans customarily disturb, though that event had not yet taken place here. There were great trees, and lesser ones. There were open places, with high grasses that shifted as breezes came, making gentle, graceful sounds as they moved. Not far from us there was a pool, with water falling from a great height and splashing into it; and, from one end of the pool, a steady flow of water that passed over great and little rocks that it made smooth. Other rocks, away from the water, were rough to the touch. Some were piled closely together, almost as by a human; though, because of the lovely imperfection of the arrangement, it was certainly by nature. Not far away, behind the falling water, was a small opening that led into a great rock ledge. It was possible to dream that a new opening into the center of the earth had been made in this place, and for us!

It was strange when we got to this place—the land sloped gently—for Moses did not make a sign to stop. We knew.

"Wow!" Lollipop said.

The sun, as it left the sky that day, made itself more beautiful than it had ever been. Long before it stole behind the hills, it changed to a deep and rich color, inviting and

friendly, comforting to stare at, filled with a blessing sent to us four apes. It was a sign that we could not overlook; even Lollipop was quieted by it.

For several days now, we had not groomed each other. There had been countless things to take our time, and many experiences. The common civilities that are a part of ape life had been forgotten and we looked terrible. The sign that the sun had given us changed our moods. It was the time to resume civil behavior. How strange it seems now that Lollipop was the first to know of this change. She had lost her timidness (or was it simple fear?) toward Moses and presented herself to him to be groomed. Moses began to spread apart Lollipop's hairs and to pick off woodland creatures that had lodged there, and to remove small pieces of skin. For a long time we groomed each other, roaming freely from one to the other for some minutes at a time. We groomed until our friend, the beautiful sun, had taken away all of the world's light and it became night. We ate some of the supplies we had carried with us.

Moses made a great noise. If there were unfriendly creatures nearby, that noise would have frightened them away. We slept without lookouts that night.

When dawn came we woke up. It is the correct time to wake up. Moses told us that hereafter we would always wake with the dawn, for that is the natural way in the faraway lands.

"It's very early," Lollipop said. "I want to sleep some more." Moses tickled Lollipop and she was wide awake in half a minute.

82

"Now we talk," Moses said.

"Is it that way in faraway lands?" I asked.

"The first hours are for talking," Moses said.

"I want to play," Lollipop said.

"Other hours are for playing," Moses said.

"I don't like talking," Lollipop said. "Besides, half of the time I don't know what you're talking about. Also, you don't talk like Dylys and Sasha."

"Lollipop!" Dylys said. "Apologize."

"Why?"

"Moses speaks the language of the faraway lands," Dylys said. "It is Sasha and I and you, too, who speak crudely."

"I speak like any other ape," Lollipop said.

"We have lost our language," I said. "Moses will teach it to us. Do as Dylys said. Apologize to Moses."

Lollipop moved slowly to Moses. She put out her hands. Moses nodded, and he rubbed the back of Lollipop's head. He also tickled her a little bit and we were all happy.

During the first hour Moses made many noises. Most were quiet ones, and each had a meaning. He explained the meanings of the various noises. Some were formal noises, meant only to establish friendliness and courtesy among apes. We practiced each one.

"The sounds make it possible to save ape-words," Moses said. "Ape-words are for great discussions."

Other sounds were for common comments that do not require discussion. There are sounds to indicate that an ape has had a long and quiet sleep; that the night has passed fitfully and was filled with terrible dreams; that an ape feels well at dawn, or badly; that an ape wishes to be left alone.

The great sounds, those that could be heard throughout the nearby territory, were for other purposes. None of us would be able to make them at first. Moses assured us that we would learn them. Those sounds, like the one Moses had made as we prepared to sleep the night before, were to warn other creatures to stay away, and to threaten enemies. Another great sound was to signal apes in other territories: sometimes in friendship and sometimes not, depending on the relationships among apes. Moses thought there would be no need to teach us this last sound, for no apes would reply here in this country.

"We must learn all the sounds, Moses," I said. "It will be important to us."

Moses nodded. He made several more great sounds, each different in subtle ways. There were sounds for alarm and aggression and extreme joy and numerous other matters. It was glorious to listen to them as Moses first made them. Sometimes he would ask us to guess the meanings of the sounds, and it was hard for us to do so. Other times he would tell us wonderful stories associated with a particular sound, and then make that sound.

"One time," Moses said, "there was a terrible drought on the savanna in a land near my own. Many months passed and the grasses and shrubs shriveled up and died. There was nothing for apes or any other creatures to eat, so they began to turn on each other. While all creatures had become weak, some were weaker than others and they were soon killed and eaten by the strongest. It was a terrible thing. Extreme things happen. When the rains finally came and the earth grew fruitful again, those apes who had survived gathered together and vowed that such acts must never again occur. As those who made this decision were the strongest of the strong, all others agreed. They pondered for many days, and concluded that their natural places in the future should not be in the savanna but in the high lands where the trees and bushes were thick. Those who were left moved to the high lands and, there, became the greatest tribe of apes in the world. My own tribe is related to them. It happens every once in a while that an ape will feel a pull to return to the savanna and will even wander off toward that part of the world. When the other apes know that one of them is gone because of this primitive need some have to be in their ancestors' lands, they have a special call. It is the dry savanna call. It sounds like this."

Moses made a long, piercing sound that filled the hills. It was a wail that chilled my blood. I could see that the hair on Lollipop's and Dylys' backs stood erect.

"An ape headed toward the savanna," Moses continued, "will always hear the dry savanna call, and will know that the other apes are giving a warning: in the savanna, death and desolation await you. Most apes return as soon as they hear the call, for the terrible time on the savanna is something even the youngest ape has heard of. Sometimes an ape cannot be restrained, however, and will go to the savanna. Apes and other creatures living on the savanna hate these visitors and frequently turn on them and brutalize them or kill them. They are able to do this because of their number, not their strength, for the strongest and brightest of the savanna apes left that place in the ancient days." Moses made the dry savanna call again, and it frightened us all.

Two, or maybe even three hours were passed that morning, with Moses teaching us the sounds. Lollipop became impatient frequently, and then Moses would tell a story about one of the sounds. As soon as a story was to be told, Lollipop listened intently. Someday that little ape would grow up and tell these stories to others, and she wanted to hear every detail. We practiced the sounds as Moses made them. Lollipop liked some of the sounds very much; her favorite sound that first day was the one that meant an ape felt badly in the morning. She made that sound over and over again and was pleased when Moses told her she made it as well as any ape in the faraway lands. Dylys and I were more hesitant than Lollipop, but Moses encouraged us and before long it seemed natural to make the sounds, even though we lacked any skill. There is a special sound to indicate approval and praise, and Moses made it often, more out of charity, I think, than as an accurate estimate. There was another sound to indicate that we had talked enough, and Moses finally made that sound.

"Now it is time to eat," Moses said. Lollipop ran toward the sacks of supplies, but Moses stopped her. "No," he said. "We'll eat some of those things for a while, but here," he said, sweeping his arm around, up and down the hill, up to the trees, and pointing to the bushes and grasses, "is where we find the berries and the leaves and the nuts that we eat."

"That stuff?" Lollipop said. "That stuff's not fit for ape consumption," she insisted.

"You'll see," Moses said.

We roamed around our new place, now and then climbing a tree. We picked at many things. Some were sweet and tasted good; others were sour to the tongue and we would spit them out. Certain pieces of bark were delicious.

When one of us found a leaf or other thing of special succulence, we called out to the others and all enjoyed the pleasant object. Lollipop lowered her head into the stream to drink water, but Moses showed her, and us, a way to cup our hands and catch the water in them and bring it up to our mouths. Lollipop had so much fun drinking in this way, and splashing what fell from her hands over her body, that it was hard to lead her away from the stream.

We spent many hours finding foods until Moses signaled that we had finished. We returned to the supply sacks.

"Are you hungry still?" Moses asked. He pointed to the sacks. It was his way of permitting them to be opened and used, but not even Lollipop moved toward them. "Later, we will eat some of the supplies before they are rotten, and no longer sweet to taste."

"That's O.K. by me," Lollipop said. Moses stared questioningly at Lollipop.

Now it was time for grooming and play. Some hours were passed in this way. It was an idle time, and pleasant in every way. From time to time one or the other of us fell asleep for short periods of time. We awoke refreshed, sometimes to tumble about, sometimes to climb a tree to look here and there at our new place and the territory that surrounded it.

In the late part of the day we moved out to eat again, though not as much as in the morning. We ate some of the supplies that we had brought with us, but they did not have the special taste of the growing things everywhere around us.

"It is time to talk again," Moses said. "The time to talk

is when you awake and before you sleep. All other talk is extra. The only occasions for other talk are for special circumstances and emergencies. There is a way to live that anyone who listens closely to the real world understands. Soon you will understand the real world, for the other creatures who live here with us are a part of it, too. Already I have seen that your birds, with their dull colors, have remained apart from the human world. They have times that are like ours. When they fly away after their morning talk, in search of food, that is a good time to take their nests and eat the eggs in them. Those eggs are delicious. Especially," Moses said, "when they are new eggs." Dylys turned from Moses. He touched her on the back. "It is natural and expected," he said. "You will see."

Moses went over some of the sounds he had introduced to us in the morning. Lollipop, Dylys and I recollected some of them very well, but others less well. It got dark and was time for sleep. Moses told us that he would make the sleep sound that would fill the world with fear. He made it. It was the sound he had made the night before. He told us where this sound had come from and what it meant to other creatures.

"Once," Moses said, "in ancient times, a weird one stalked the earth. It was not ape, or human, or creature that any other would have known. It always lurked apart from others, ready to spring on and devour the first innocent stray. It made no distinctions among creatures. Any lone creature was suitable to the weird one. Many innocents met their end in the clutches of it. Each creature, including apes, decided to make a sign, or a noise, that would frighten the weird one away. The homebound creatures devised signs and noises; flying creatures made noises;

underwater creatures disappeared under rocks and the soft surfaces available to them. All nature conspired against the weird one. But the weird one still exists. It is important to make the sounds and give the signs that will fill the weird one with fear, so that it will keep its distance. Otherwise, it will take strays and any casuals that happen to pass and will devastate them. The weird one roams the world. The weird one can be in many places at the same time. Some say that the weird one wears many disguises, and it is possible that that is true. An ape never sleeps at night without first warning away the weird one."

Each day passed like all the others, and after a time it became possible to imagine that we were in the faraway lands. The earth was generous, and by the time we were finished with the supplies we had brought, we no longer needed them. Moses taught us how to crack open nuts for the sweet meats inside. It was easy to accomplish this with the right stone, one that wasn't so heavy that it would crush the nut completely, and yet heavy enough to break it open.

"Ouch!" Lollipop said each time she tried to break open nuts. She did not learn to do it easily, always smashing hard on her other hand. We agreed that we would open the nuts Lollipop gathered to assure that she not mutilate her hand by mistake. "I'll learn when I'm bigger," she promised.

It was true that Lollipop would get this skill soon enough. Moses taught us yet another skill. There were many small mounds throughout the territory. Inside, not too far from the surface, some sweet ants lived. We got them in large numbers by shoving sticks into the mounds and leaving the sticks there for many minutes. When we pulled them out they would be covered with the little creatures, and we ate them as a special treat. They are most delicious to the taste, though it was tough on the ants.

During the talking times at dawn and before sleep, we began to use sounds frequently and naturally. As our skills increased, Moses made new sounds, explaining the meanings; so that with each day we learned the language of our people, and their legends as well.

One day, while we were wandering about getting our food, Moses made a piercing sound that he had never made before. Dylys and I ran to him, as he kept making the sound again and again. There was great alarm in it. He was next to the great pool into which the water from above falls. There, some feet away from him, was Lollipop, who had slipped over the edge of the pool and was beating frantically in the water. In a matter of seconds she would go under, as would Moses if he went unaided to save her: apes cannot swim. I grabbed hold of Moses' hand in an instant; Dylys took my other hand. With Moses as a great anchor I plunged into the pool, and so did Dylys. If we pulled Moses with us, we would be drowned in minutes, all four of us. Our efforts would end in this pool. Dylys grasped Lollipop as she was about to sink, and Moses pulled us all to land. We paused briefly, relieved.

Except Lollipop made no noise. Nor were her eyes open. Moses grabbed her legs and shook her; water poured out of her mouth, and she seemed to squirm. Moses stopped shaking her. We laid her on the grass next to the pool and stood looking at her, fearful that she might have taken in too much water. Dylys bent over Lollipop, feeling her body. She turned her over, and more water poured from her mouth. Now it was certain that she was squirming, and finally her eyes opened.

"Am I here?" Lollipop said.

"Yes," Dylys said.

Lollipop turned over to look at Dylys. "What happened?" she said.

"It's all right now," Dylys said.

"Are you sure?" Lollipop asked. She tried to sit up but fell back. Dylys lifted her onto her own back and we went to high and dry ground to watch the life come back into Lollipop. And in some minutes she came around well. "I saw a fish," Lollipop said. "I wanted to hold it."

"Moses was nearby," Dylys said.

Lollipop stared at Moses for a long time, finally moving to him. She touched Moses all over, every place on his body from the top of his head down to his feet. She did the same with me and with Dylys, and then returned to Moses to touch him and groom him for many minutes.

Moses then told us the story of the sound he had made. It was the ape-in-the-water sound. "It is made only for the bravest apes," Moses began, rubbing the back of Lollipop's head, "for only a brave ape would go close to big waters."

"Thank you," Lollipop said.

"In the most ancient times," Moses said, "so ancient that no ape can guess how long ago it might have been, apes ruled the world. There was no creature of any sort whose power came close to that of the apes. Wherever there was life, all living things honored and feared apes. Any living thing that did not have proper respect or that challenged

91

apes in any way was eliminated. With such power, apes came to accept themselves as invincible. They believed they would rule the world forever.

"In those ancient days there was one judge, a creature no ape had ever seen but who lived in the sky and traveled from place to place in great clouds made for that purpose, and in this way saw everything that happened in the world. In their pride, apes believed that the great judge was, of course, a supreme ape, who would naturally favor apes in all things. Millenniums, perhaps ages, passed as the great judge saw, first, what good things apes did in the world. The judge was benign and favored those with worthy objectives, for at the beginning, as the apes separated themselves by their own lofty intentions from other creatures, apes did, indeed, make the world a better place. However, as nothing escaped the attention of the great judge, in due course it became clear to this being that the good apes who had noble aims had been succeeded by two others who were tyrants, ruling the world arbitrarily, secure that the great judge, above, was the greatest of their own. The tyrant apes even used the name of the great judge to explain and justify all that they did. With the passing of even more time, the apes removed themselves farther and farther from their original purposes and natures. In changing the world, they had changed themselves.

"A century or more passed, as the great judge sought to give the apes time to change their tyrannical ways. In the next century, the judge sent signs: apes turned on each other, for example, not content to rule over all other creatures in the world. Instead of accepting the signs as good counsel, the apes became even more arbitrary and ruthless. Wars raged, sometimes between apes and other creatures, with the apes always victorious, but just as frequently between apes and apes. This last kind of war taxed every ape's ingenuity. Devices tested successfully on other creatures were used, ape against ape, in battles that became fiercer and fiercer with the passing of time.

" 'They will come to their senses now,' the great judge thought. It was a generous assessment, but proved incorrect. With the heaviest heart conceivable, the great judge concluded that the time of the ape must pass.

" 'There will be more waters on earth,' the great judge pronounced. This is how the oceans, the seas and the greatest rivers came into existence. Before, the earth had been mostly land, with waters enough for all who lived but no great mass of waters. 'Creatures will be separated from each other, and will develop in their particular ways. Creatures will make an attempt to live in harmony, one with the other, with no single creature greater than any other. No creature will dominate another, for the apes have shown us the extremes to which domination leads. The world is an unhappy place because of apes.'

"As apes heard the great judge, they asked if the judge was not itself an ape.

" 'The judge is not an ape, nor any other creature. Nor is the judge great. The judge hopes to be just.' Then the waters came. It seemed, for a time, that the world would give itself over to the waters, but this was not at all the case. Lands were abundant.

"At first apes did not understand what had happened to the world, nor did the other creatures on it. In time, however, creatures found that they could attack apes, and flee from them to the waters. Apes would pursue attackers vigorously, even into the waters. Other creatures were able to live in the waters, to swim in flight. But when an ape entered the waters, the ape drowned in minutes.

"In this way, many apes disappeared. In certain parts of the world where they had ruled absolutely, they came no longer to exist. And in other parts of the world, they came to accept themselves as part of, not rulers of, the world."

"Is the great judge still looking over things?" Lollipop asked.

"Yes," Moses said.

Our routine continued as before, but Lollipop did not feel the joy in it that she had before. Her brush with near-drowning made her timid in numerous ways. She would never wander too far from me or Dylys or, especially, Moses. She groomed Moses on any possible occasion, and while it was not an obsession with her, Lollipop wanted always to see that Moses was well taken care of. She took special delight in bringing an abundance of leaves to make Moses' sleeping nest as comfortable as it could be.

"You are such a big ape," Lollipop said, "that we might run out of leaves for your nest. But don't worry. We'll always find enough for you." Moses nodded agreeably. He was most indulgent toward Lollipop, and tickled her a a lot, as well.

A change was coming, and, except for Lollipop, we felt uneasy. Dylys would go off by herself for some hours. She frequently went to the cave behind the falling water and sat there alone in the dark.

One day it was certain that the change had come. Dylys

had become ripe. It was not the first time for her. Lollipop stared with amazement at the great redness that signaled that Dylys had ripened. Now, this time, she would be able to give birth to her own ape. She would be a good ape mother, but it frightened her nevertheless.

Some time passed. Dylys did not present herself to either Moses or me. We stayed away from her so as not to scare her even more. I had copulated many times before and so, certainly, had Moses. Moses and I took to staring at each other for many minutes. Once we sat looking at each other for a whole hour.

"I will not fight you," I said to Moses finally. "It is unnecessary. I would lose."

Moses nodded. He came to me and I held out my hands to him. He bit my hands gently. As Moses was my brother, and I his, in our minds one was not greater than the other.

Moses went off with Dylys.

"What's happening?" Lollipop demanded to know. I explained to her that Moses and Dylys would copulate many times in the next days and that there would be another ape in our family. I also explained to her that someday she would copulate, too, and become a mother ape. "Where is the little ape?" Lollipop asked when Moses and Dylys came back. We all ape-laughed, all except Lollipop. "Sasha said there would be a little ape. I'm tired of being the littlest."

4

JOINED

DYLYS' ripe time passed. While our daily routine during those weeks was much as it had been before the ripeness, there was always a time when Moses and Dylys went off together, leaving behind Lollipop and myself. Lollipop became resigned to having to wait for the new ape.

"Why don't you make a little ape with Dylys, too? Then there would be two," Lollipop said.

It was a painful question for me to answer in a way that would make sense to Lollipop. Moses had indicated, after a proper interval, that it would be right for me to copulate with Dylys, for that is the customary way in the faraway lands. He had been first, and would continue to be first, but I was, after all, his brother. Dylys looked away when Moses made the suggestion, and so did I. There was nothing for me, but to present my hands to Moses for him to bite, always gently. Those were hard days for me and I was glad when they ended. With the great redness gone, it became easier for Dylys and me to resume our friendship, even while Moses did not understand my unnatural reticence.

"It is best that an infant ape have many fathers," Moses said. "In that way, if something terrible happens to one of them, all the others stand in his place. That is the natural way. Dylys should be with many apes during her ripeness, for after she has her little ape it will be some years before it is time for her to turn red again and have another ape. She should enjoy herself and the protection of many apes, too.

"In the ancient days," Moses continued, "before the great judge made waters cover much of the earth, it was the custom, they say, for apes to mate with only one other ape. There are creatures, not apes, in the faraway lands who cling to that practice still, but they were never powerful like apes. After the waters came, and millions of apes drowned, and the judge saw to it that apes would no longer remain dominant, it became necessary for all male apes, even lesser males, to take the father's part. Otherwise, there would have been fights between families, and in the end, perhaps, no apes at all. So, you see, when there is only one family, all are responsible for the safety and good fortune of all others in the family. That is a lesson the great judge left for apes, even though apes had to discover it for themselves."

"Well," I said to Moses, "you are the father of Dylys' baby."

"Yes," he said.

As the days passed, it was as though there had never been a university and a gymnasium in the past, filled with apes and scientists, and graduate students and instruments for testing and examining. Except, one night I had a dream about Otto, the little natural ape who had been

100

the first selected to be led to the laboratory where all of us had been examined. Otto was playing with numerous basketballs, and with breathtaking dexterity. A great crowd surrounded him. They cheered him mightily as he threw first one, then another, and still another basketball through the air and through hoops that hung off walls. The crowd got into a frenzy as Otto tossed the basketballs through the hoops. There were other apes here and there on the basketball floor with Otto, but they were indistinct to me, for Otto was so much the star of the game, no other ape could be noticed. It was an exciting event to watch, for in addition to Otto's flawless toss, the young ape moved about the gymnasium floor with a grace and speed that were totally admirable. I looked, in my dream, at the crowd cheering each of Otto's moves. Most of them were humans. I saw the old female scientist with a stick, the one who had first approached Moses and rubbed his head. I saw Crossley M. Winkle, the graduate student who had befriended my friend Myrtle. Even though I had never met Winkle, I knew her because she wore a tee shirt with this legend printed on it: Crossley M. Winkle, A Friend. And I saw numerous apes cheering, too. They were sitting with the humans. There was Myrtle, next to Winkle. Solomon was nodding his approval toward Otto, though he could not bring himself to applaud or cheer. Hortense was bursting with ape-pride. Other apes from my past were there, too. I saw my mother. It was the first time I had seen her since I left San Diego, and I called out to her. "It's Sasha," I said, "your Sasha! Do you remember me? I know this little flash, Otto. We were part of the same experiment! One day we will all play on the court with Otto, Mother! You'll see! It will be just as Myrtle said it would be! There will be no problems! Experiments will stop and we'll all be basketball players! Do you remember your Sasha?"

"Sasha," I heard a voice say, "Sasha."

I woke with a start. I sat up in my nest, and almost fell out of it. "What?" I said.

"It's all right, Sasha," Dylys said. "You made many noises in your sleep. You woke us up." Lollipop was spread along Dylys' back; she was staring wide-eyed at me. I looked to the ground, and could see Moses sitting under my nest; he also looked at me intently. I jumped to the ground, next to Moses. He put an arm around me, and rubbed my head. He kissed me. Dylys, Lollipop still on her back, jumped next to me. She kissed me, too. Lollipop pushed away both Moses and Dylys so she could kiss me. It was nearly morning, so we sat together on the ground, huddled together, arms wrapped around each other and bellies close, through the cold gray part that follows the night, until at last the sun and real daylight came.

"I had a dream," I said, breaking our silence. We moved together, closer than before.

Some days passed after the night of my dream, and all was as it had been before. The sun, we noticed, came up later in the morning each day, and left the sky earlier in the evening. The grasses and leaves that had been so sweet to our tastes seemed somehow less sweet; the berries were hard or had disappeared; the nuts were dry. The earth did not seem bountiful.

Dylys saw him first. He stood on the ledge above us, next to the stream that tumbled over that ledge into the pool below.

"Human!" Dylys said. She made one of the danger sounds that Moses had taught us. We rushed to trees nearby, and hid among branches. Several minutes passed. At the end of a half hour, Moses jumped to the ground and moved cautiously among low trees and undergrowth toward the waterfall. He edged through bushes next to the waterfall and peered up. He made the danger sound Dylys had made before. The human was still there, and Moses rushed back to the trees where we were hidden.

"He just stands there, looking in our direction," Moses said quietly. "I think he knows where we are hiding."

Lollipop was clinging closely to Dylys, who tried to soothe her. "It's all right. Get on my back," Dylys urged. But Lollipop clung to Dylys' front side, so that Dylys could not move easily.

"He must not find where we are hiding," I said. I jumped to the ground and moved around the big pool of water at the bottom of the waterfall. I followed the stream that spilled from the pool down the great hill until it came to a part that was mostly big rocks. I crossed there, filled with fears, for if I fell into the stream and it carried me into deeper waters where there were no big rocks, I would fall victim to the curse on apes made by the great judge in ancient times. But I reached the other side of the stream successfully, and made my way up the hill toward the other side of the pool. There was a clearing up there, with high grasses and very few trees. I looked up. The human was standing on the ledge, next to the waterfall. He could come down the ledge now, and we would be on the same side of the pool below. I lumbered slowly into the clearing, and sat. I looked up at the human, who stared down at me. I began to pull at some of the grass around me, putting some in my mouth and chewing it. While I was intent on this activity, with my head slightly bowed, I kept my eyes on the human above. If he came down the ledge, Moses and Dylys and Lollipop could flee, or hide themselves in the opening behind the waterfall, while the human approached only me. I did not know what I would do if he came near. Would I run away? Or attack him? Or wait for him to attack me? What if he had a weapon and attacked me from a distance so that I could do nothing? What if he killed me? All these questions filled my mind until I saw that the human began to lower himself over the ledge. He grabbed little bushes that stuck out here and there on the ledge as he lowered one foot onto a narrow protrusion, steadied himself momentarily there, and then lowered his other foot to another protrusion. He moved steadily, his belly pressed against the ledge, pausing only three times to look over his shoulder to see if I was sitting where I had been in the moments before. I sat, munching grass, staring at him on his descent. I also looked across the pool to see if the others were fleeing, but I could not take my eyes too long from the human and, so, did not know if they stayed hidden in the trees or had fled for safety.

The human reached the bottom of the ledge. He turned. He stood quietly, staring at me. He was not a scientist. His hair fell long down his back; he had tied it together with a piece of vine at his neck, so that as it fell it looked more like a tail than a human head of hair. His tee shirt and worn blue pants were torn here and there, and he wore no shoes. He had a drowsy degree of about 25%. His face was bearded, and his eyes—clear and blue—did not leave my own. I stopped munching on grass. After some moments the human took steps toward me. As he approached, the sun fell on a piece of metal fixed to a leather handle fastened to a loop on his pants: it was a short, sharp knife. My fears grew, but I would not take my eyes from the human or move away from him. He came within six feet of me before stopping. He sat, crossing his legs in front of him, sitting on his feet. He drew his knife, and still I did not move. I watched as he cut three pieces of tall grass, put the end of one of them in his mouth and laid the other two in front of him, closer to me than himself. He put his knife back into its loop. I took the two grass strands. We sat, munching grass, staring into each other's eyes. He did not smile; I liked it that he did not smile.

As this time between me and the human lengthened, and as neither he nor I gave fear signs, he edged closer to me when he uncrossed his legs. He put his hands out toward me, so that I might look at them. I moved forward, and took hold of each of his hands in turn. I kept my eyes on his, too, looking rapidly at his hands and then back into his eyes. Finally I raised each of his hands to my mouth and bit on them, as gently as Moses would bite on my own.

"Oh," the human said. He laughed when he said it and fell on his back. It was a quick movement that startled me at first, though it was clear immediately that the human was happy; his laugh was not a nervous one, but a laugh from the heart. Apes know many human laughs, and laughs from the heart are the best kind. Smiles that follow such laughs are agreeable, too, for they resemble in no way customary human smiles. The human raised himself on his elbow and stared at me more. "Oh, my God," he said, laughing again. He moved closer to me and I had no inclination to back away. He touched me on my head, and ran his hands over my front side, all the time laughing. He reached some tickle places, and as he gave me pleasure, I tickled him, too. We were both, in our human and ape ways, laughing and having a good time, so I lay flat on the ground and let him tickle me a lot. I put my arm around his neck, and with the other hand pulled at his tee shirt. He took it off, knotting it around one of his arms, so I ran my hand up and down over his skin. There was hair on it, but it was in patches here and there and no more than is on a baby ape. That is why humans wear clothes: to cover their hairlessness.

I nearly forgot myself, and why I had come to this side of the pool, when I could see that the human had moved away from me and was sitting up. I looked across the pool and saw Moses and Dylys and Lollipop next to it, looking at the human and me. I rubbed the back of the human's head, reassuringly, took him by the hand and led him down the hill to where the big rocks made it easy for me to cross the stream. We crossed together; the human knew my fear as by instinct, and held my hand tight in his own. I led him up the hill on the other side of the stream.

"This is Man," I said to Moses when I reached my three companions. I led the human to Moses, who sat, Dylys next to him with Lollipop on her back, staring at the human. "I think he is not like the other humans we have known," I said. I pushed the human forward. I took his hands and presented them to Moses. After a moment, Moses bit the human's hands in his gentle way, and rubbed the human's head. He moved the human's hands to Dylys and to Lollipop. Each of us apes kept feeling his skin. It was sad that he had so little hair, and needed a tee shirt and pants to protect him. Lollipop pulled at the long tail of hair falling down the human's back. He laughed his good and genuine pleasure laugh and offered his arms to Lollipop to hold her. She sprang from Dylys' back into the human's arms. Lollipop spent many minutes, then, unfastening the vine that held the human's tail hair together and twisting the loose hair hanging from the human's head around her fingers, hands, arms and her neck. We laughed together.

The human lived with us. He could not sleep in the trees as we did, so when he gathered leaves to make his nest at night, he spread them on the ground under our trees. It was dangerous to sleep on the ground because of the roaming night creatures, so we knew that the human had courage. Moses always made the night sound to keep away those creatures. Each day the human left us for a few hours, and once for four hours. When it happened the first time, we did not know that he would return, so all four of us apes were sad. When he came back he brought many tasty grasses and foods from the lower parts of the hills. The things he brought with him did not grow at great heights, and they were sweeter to the taste than anything we had eaten for several weeks. The human found a cloth sack on one of his trips below, and so was able to fill it with many foods. We began to store foods in a dark corner of the cave behind the waterfall.

The human hardly ever talked. I tried to get him to talk. I put my hand in his mouth two times, and drew it out in a way that would indicate that if he talked we would understand him. He only laughed. He was extremely affectionate, and held each of us close to him whenever we came near. Lollipop took to riding on his back, more, now, than on Dylys'. I moved to follow the human on one of his trips below, but he let me accompany him only a short distance. Then we sat. He put his arm around my neck and I put my arm around his. We sat in this way for ten or twelve minutes, and I put my hand under his tee shirt and gave him some rubs. He laughed. I pulled at his pants, so he took them off and I felt the bottom part of his body. There was hair there, but not like an ape's; I held his genitals, examining them closely, and rubbed my hands over his buttocks and legs. He kept laughing, patted me on the head and put on his pants. He motioned for me to go back up the hill, so I did that. On the next day, Lollipop crept away just as soon as Man—for he kept the name I had first given him—took the sack to go below. She followed him for some distance, until he discovered her and brought her back to us. Lollipop was glad to get the long ride on Man's back.

We wondered why it was that Man did not speak ape language. He was filled with merits. It seemed unlikely to us that he did not speak our language.

"He is brave," Moses said.

"He provides for us," Dylys said.

"He is the friendliest and most open of any human," I said.

"I love Man," Lollipop said.

Man listened closely each dawn as we made our morning noises and our words. He joined us as we roamed about looking for food to eat, even though he kept bringing us more than enough. He played with us when we played. He slept when we slept. He was our brother.

It was cold in the nights, now, and in the mornings as we awoke, even colder. The green leaves that had tasted the best had begun to take on other colors. They were yellow at first, and then orange and red. On many trees, the leaves would fall to the ground. This made a great and easy supply for our sleeping nests, but we sensed that our food was fast disappearing. Everything around us was brittle and tasteless, so we began to rely mostly on the foods Man brought from below. There was plenty each day, and plenty more to store in the cave. Nevertheless, it mystified Moses and Dylys and me that the earth in our area was changing in a way none of us understood. One day we saw that many of the trees had no leaves on them at all. Their branches were as before; they stuck out, strong and sturdy. So it was only the leaves that fell, not the branches.

"It is not like this in the faraway lands," Moses said. "There are always growing things to eat."

One day a deer ran into our area and drank from the pool. We were nearby and it moved away in haste as soon as it saw us. Within the hour two more deer came, and then another. They moved on as quickly as they arrived.

Man motioned us to come together. Lollipop thought it would be for a game of some kind, so she climbed on Man's back and began to tickle him. Man swung her off his back and held her close in front of him. We stared at him closely, for there was a grave look in his eyes.

That was when we first heard the noises. They came from a long distance away, many miles perhaps. They were loud, sharp and irregular. Man closed his eyes each time a

109

noise came. Moses was the first to understand, and then I understood.

"What is it?" Dylys asked. Then I remembered the first thing Dylys had done that remained in my mind. It was when she gave the prayer of thanks after a meal in the gymnasium. I remembered her shyness, and her fears and perceptions, well.

"Those are noises humans make with their weapons," I told her.

"Will they come here?" she asked.

"It is too high and far away," I said.

"Weapons?" Lollipop said.

"They will not come this high," I said.

Moses nodded gravely. Man kept looking from one to the other of us. He held Lollipop even more closely. She squirmed, and put her belly against Man's belly, her arms around his neck.

The sharp noises went on for many hours, almost until darkness came. They stopped, but throughout the night many creatures passed through our area. Most were deer, but there were others, too. We lay protected in our nests, but Man sat on the ground next to our trees, awake through the night. At dawn, instead of waiting for our morning talk, Man brought us together, as he had on the day before. When it was daylight, with the sun on the horizon, he led us to the cave. The noises of the day before had begun again, and while far away, they were more distinct; and they came more often. Man took Moses to the food stored in the dark, and pointed to it again and again. He rubbed the back of Moses' head, and Moses sat next to the pile of food. He motioned for Dylys and Lollipop to sit next to Moses. He rubbed them, and Lollipop began to whimper.

Man held her close and kissed her several times before handing her to Dylys to hold; it occurred to me for the first time that Man probably thought Dylys was Lollipop's mother.

Man walked with me to the front of the cave. He made many signs to indicate that we should stay in the cave. He put his hands to his chest and then to mine. I took these signs to mean that he would be back in a while, and that the noises would cease. I made the same signs to him. I told him in ape language that we would await his return, and that I understood that we should stay in the cave, where there was plenty of food. He began to move out of the cave, but I grabbed his hand. I rubbed his head and neck, and he rubbed mine.

"This may be the cave that leads to the center of the earth," I told Man, hoping that he would understand ape language at last. "In the ancient times and the faraway lands, there was such an opening and only chosen apes were allowed to make that journey. If this is such a cave, and Moses and Dylys and Lollipop and I are chosen, we will wait for Man before making the journey. For Man is especially chosen, too. Man is our brother. It is as Lollipop says, we love Man. I wish you could understand me." I pushed my hand under Man's tee shirt and rubbed his front and his back; I rubbed his genitals and buttocks; I put my lips to each of his feet, for that is the proper way to wish that your brother have a safe trip and a swift return to his family. He left.

The noises from the weapons continued through the day. We occasionally went a few feet out of the cave, especially when some unaccustomed sound was close: it was usually a deer; once it was a small family of mountain cats. None paused long, other than to drink from the pool or the stream nearby. None came close to the cave. By darkness, Man had not returned, though, as on the night before, the noises stopped.

Another day passed, then a third and a fourth. Each was like the one before it, though now it seemed the noises were closer, much closer, than before. When we slept, it was agreed that Moses and Dylys and I would take turns standing guard at the entrance to the cave. It was as it had been on those first nights of flight from the gymnasium. There was plenty of food, though we did not have much hunger for it.

On the fifth day many deer and other creatures ran into our area, sometimes pausing, sometimes not. If they paused, it was to wait for their young, who did not move fast and who did not understand why it was necessary to keep moving. The sounds from the weapons were nearby, now, and it was strange and unusual for Moses and Dylys and me to sit idly in the cave as the terrifying noises came close. Lollipop kept herself far back in the dark. She had found that some of the food Man had left us would roll when pushed, and spent many hours rolling these foods from one place to the other in the cave.

"Look at that waterfall! That sure is some sight," a human said.

"Man!" Lollipop shrieked. She ran past the rest of us

out of the cave. Dylys was the first to understand what had happened and began to run after Lollipop.

"Je . . . sus!" the human outside the cave said. "What the hell is that?"

"Lollipop!" Dylys called out. "Come back. It is not Man!" I grabbed Dylys, to keep her from running after Lollipop.

It happened in seconds. The human who had talked dropped a dead deer laced upside down to a pole that he carried with another human, and made a terrible noise with his weapon. The noise ended in Lollipop, who jumped into the air and fell next to the waterfall. "Man!" Lollipop called out. "Man!"

Moses made the dry savanna call and ran from the cave.

"Je . . . sus!" the human said again. He fired his weapon once more, and then again, and again.

"Moses!" I yelled. "Lollipop!" I kept hold of Dylys, who called out to Moses and Lollipop herself.

Moses fell next to Lollipop.

"Get the hell out of here!" the human said. He and his companion ran down the hill away from the pool. "Je . . . sus!" I kept hearing them yell.

They had left behind the dead deer. Moses lay next to Lollipop, and as Dylys and I ran out of the cave, he made a great sound. It was his last sound. Blood came from him in several places, for many noises had been made at him. His great black eyes stared up at me, and I remembered the first time I had remarked to myself on them, in the dark gymnasium as he gazed at the strange world in which he had found himself. Lollipop, wide-eyed, frightened, put one of her fingers into a hole a noise had made in her, and placed that finger in her mouth. She looked at Dylys.

Then at me. She closed her eyes and she fell back on Moses. There they were: dead. A deer unknown to us, still strapped to a pole; and two apes, great Moses from the faraway lands, and just as great Lollipop.

We cried. What else was there for us, Dylys and me, to do?

Nobody else came. Man did not come back. Where was Man?

One day, days after the noises killed Moses and Lollipop, I told Dylys that we could not stay any longer in the cave.

"Yes," she said. "I know."

"We will find another place," I said.

She looked around at the trees. Most were leafless now. "No," she said.

On the next morning, we got up with the dawn. The noises from the humans' weapons had not been heard for some days, and the earth seemed as safe as it had seemed before those noises began. A deer would pass through our area, and then another and several more, all going back to the lower lands. We would look at them in silence, as they looked at us in the same way. We knew, these deer and other creatures that passed, that the humans had come and gone. We had passed together through the time of the humans, those of us who looked at one another. So we joined the slow procession out of the hills to the lands below.

How long had it been since Moses and Dylys and Lollipop and I had made the journey to the favored place, where for many, many weeks life had been joyous? It was hard for me to remember. I held Dylys' hand tight in my own.

"How long?" I asked.

"It was a long time ago, and it seems not to have been that long ago."

"Yes," I said.

We walked over many hills, sleeping together each night in the same nest. Neither Dylys nor I had shared nests before, for we were both too big to lie together at ease in the same nest. We accommodated ourselves. One day we got to the hill that overlooked the university, the very hill where we had been together for our first rest. The sun was still high in the sky when we got to our old place, so there was no reason to pause there if we were going back to the gymnasium.

"Stay," Dylys said.

"Yes," I said.

That day, and into the night, Dylys and I talked for many hours about the faraway lands. We talked of the matters Moses had told us: of the great judge and the waters, of the weird one who roamed the night, of the calls and their purposes, of the ways to be an ape. We talked of Lollipop. Of Moses. And of Man. We groomed each other. As before, Dylys and I cried.

The next day we left the last hill and crept down it past houses and other human places. We came at last to the university. It was early in the day. No humans walked about. I remembered the frightening night when we had left the gymnasium, and how filled with mysteries and

115

dangers the trees nearby had seemed. Dylys and I took no notice of them now. We lumbered, together, toward the gymnasium.

We got to the door that had been our escape to the outside. There was a tree near it. I led Dylys to that tree. She began to climb it, but I pulled her back to the ground.

"Sit here, Dylys," I said. She sat next to me, against the tree. I put my hand on her belly. "Moses is inside you," I said. "Someday there will be many great stories to tell that little ape." I called out the dry savanna call. Now everything that would happen would be in the hands of humans. Whatever it would be, Dylys and I would remember forever Moses and Lollipop, and would hope that Man is not lost.

Format by Kohar Alexanian
Set in 11 pt Caledonia
Composed, printed and bound by The Haddon Craftsmen, Inc.
HARPER & ROW, PUBLISHERS, INCORPORATED